DARK ENERGY

ALSO BY ROBISON WELLS

VARIANT

FEEDBACK

BLACKOUT

DEAD ZONE

GOING DARK: A BLACKOUT NOVELLA
(available as an ebook)

ROBISON WELLS

An Imprint of HarperCollinsPublishers

HarperTeen is an imprint of HarperCollins Publishers.

Dark Energy

www.epicreads.com

Library of Congress Control Number: 2015938999
ISBN 978-0-06-227505-9 (trade bdg.)

Typography by Erin Fitzsimmons
16 17 18 19 20 CG/RRDH 10 9 8 7 6 5 4 3 2 1
❖
First Edition

To the McNeills,

To Richard, who changed my world in one evening's conversation

To Lisa, who welcomed me with open arms

To Evelyn, who is always Evelyn

To Johnboy, who will always be John

PROLOGUE

Want to hear something freaky?

Go outside and look at the night sky. Assuming you're not in a big city, you should see quite a few stars—in the neighborhood of a few thousand. If you have a good set of binoculars, you can increase that to 200,000. If you're using a telescope in an observatory, you can see more than a billion.

A billion. That's a freakload of stars.

But wait, it gets better.

The Milky Way alone has 400 billion stars. And that's just one galaxy. There are more than 170 billion galaxies. If 170 billion galaxies each have 400 billion stars . . .

A septillion. That's one followed by twenty-four zeros. 1,000,000,000,000,000,000,000,000.

So, a freakload of stars.

But you know what else is out there?

Dark energy. Dark matter. We call it dark because we can't see it, like, at all. We can't see it, we don't know what it is, we don't know where it came from, and yet it makes up 96 percent of the matter in the universe.

That's right: 96 percent of the stuff of the universe is dark, inexplicable *something.*

The astronomer Carl Sagan said once, "Somewhere, something incredible is waiting to be known."

This story isn't about dark energy, except to say there is a ton of stuff in the universe that we don't understand.

Sometimes it lands here.

ONE

The aliens were probably as pissed off about landing in the Midwest as I was. I can't imagine they actually intended to set down in Iowa and then skid two hundred fifty miles north to Minnesota. The ship's cockpit was probably full of aliens saying "dammit" a lot—or whatever the alien equivalent is—and then looking out the windows to say, "Seriously, Captain? This is it?"

Not that I have anything against the Midwest. It's just that I'm supposed to live in Florida, in Miami. The Magic City. *Not* in Minneapolis. The Mill City. A city that is as far from any ocean as it's possible to be. (I haven't done the math, but it sounds right, doesn't it?) But I didn't really have a say in the matter. Before the dust had even settled over the crash site, my dad had enrolled me in the Minnetonka School for the Gifted and Talented so that he wouldn't have to leave me behind while he traveled to Minnesota. Dad was the director of special projects at NASA, at the Kennedy Space Center, and if there was anything that qualified as a special project, this was it. Aliens landing in the heartland. Pretty special.

I swear, I was on the private plane, my bag packed with three shirts, an extra pair of boots, and my laptop, before Dad even told me Minnetonka was a boarding school. He seemed legitimately surprised that I didn't know, as if I had missed some memo.

"It's just us, Dad," I told him. "Your secretary doesn't keep me in her inner circle."

"And that's exactly why you need a boarding school, Alice," he said, opening his laptop despite the fact that we hadn't taken off yet. That's what being in a NASA-owned airplane does to you, especially when the world's in crisis and you're flying toward a UFO crash site. "I'm not going to have time to take care of you—and don't even start with the 'you never have time for me' stuff. You never have time for me either. Just last week I suggested that we go to a movie—that new one with what's-his-name—and you said you were too busy."

"I *was* busy," I said. "The cat's in the cradle. 'I'm gonna be like you, Dad. You know I'm gonna be like you.'"

"You're breaking my heart. I made sure the school is coed. Would a terrible father do that?"

"So you're not only getting rid of me, you're trying to marry me off? I'm only seventeen."

"You've got me. Seventeen-year-olds can probably get married in Minnesota," he said. "I hereby give my consent. Try to find a nice doctor or something."

"I bet this school is full of aspiring doctors," I said with a grimace.

"Or politicians. It came highly recommended by some of the big names in Washington."

"Since when do you know big names in Washington?"

"Aly, have you forgotten I'm in charge of special projects for NASA? Seriously, I don't think you realize how important I am."

"I'll try to salute more often."

He leaned over and kissed my head, then turned back to his computer. I pulled out my phone to look up Minnetonka. As the page loaded, I wondered which category I fell into: gifted or talented. I got decent enough grades, but gifted? I'd never been accused of that before. I could play the piano when I was forced to, which wasn't very often. So maybe talented?

Once the website loaded, I was treated to pictures of rolling hills and huge green lawns. Some of the buildings looked brand new—all steel and glass—while others were full of gray stone and red brick. Smiling kids stood on the steps of the main building, wearing their uniforms—skirts, white oxford shirts, green sweaters. The boys wore ties. Five of the six kids in the picture were white, and four of them had blond hair. I considered the lone black boy. Was one-sixth of the school's population really black, or had they nabbed him for the picture to fill the diversity requirement?

I wondered what they'd think about me—my mom was Navajo, and I am brown-skinned and black-haired. And although I am by no means a rebel, I dyed my hair before we left Miami. As long as I was the new girl—the new Navajo girl—I might as well be the new Navajo girl with the blue streak in her hair. Dad hated it, of course, but he tolerated it, saying I was just going through a disobedient phase, which is normal during periods of high stress. I told him his mom was going through a phase. Touché.

I glanced at my dad's computer. His background wall-paper was a picture of the crash site.

"Funny-shaped spaceship," I said. "It looks like a giant Duracell battery."

"It all has to do with gravity. Build a cylindrical ship, set it spinning, and you create artificial gravity. People are walk-ing around the inside of the ship, kind of like a big hamster wheel, but not. There's more to it than that, but that's the important part. *Centripetal Force for Dummies*."

"Gee, thanks, Dad." I tried to imagine walking on the inside of the ship and eventually coming back to the same place where I'd started. It seemed so not *Star Wars*. "So inside it's all jumbled up, right?"

"Hmm?"

"If the ship is designed to be spinning all the time, and now it's not spinning anymore, everything inside must be screwed up, right? Some people are lying on the ceiling, or if there are curved hallways, then everyone is piling up at the bottom."

"Smart," he said, though he sounded distracted.

"I'm going to need more clothes," I told him, as he opened a spreadsheet. "I don't think I have an appropriate number of sweaters for a Minnesota winter."

He didn't look away from his screen. "You've always been very handy with a credit card. Have you heard they have the Mall of America in Minnesota? It's like America, but in mall form."

"Did it exterminate all the indigenous malls?"

He gave me a waffling hand, like my joke was half good. "My point is, there's a mall that has a roller coaster in it and an aquarium and probably a bunch of clothing stores and maybe even an Orange Julius. I'm sure you'll find a creative way to spend money."

I leaned over, pushing my shoulder into his. "And what about Bluebell?"

"She'll be sent to a nice, loving home. On a farm, maybe."

"Daddy," I said, pulling out the big guns. "Darling

Daddy. You wouldn't leave me in a big place all alone without Bluebell."

He sighed. "My assistant has already made the arrangements. Bluebell will get to ride on a nice big truck, and soon you'll have her all to yourself again."

I sat back in my chair and picked up my Diet Coke. "Thanks, Daddy."

Bluebell was a BMW 550i Gran Turismo. It was exactly the kind of thing that my mother would have had a stroke about, had she not already had a stroke and died when I was eight. I try not to be callous about her death, but, to be honest, she should have stopped smoking. Her stroke was her fault, so she doesn't get a say in the fast car that my dad bought for me when I got my driver's license.

As for the car, yes, it was too expensive. But there are perks to coming from money. Dad's job, while good, is not the ultimate source of our income. That honor belongs to our annual pilgrimage to the ancestral Goodwin homeland in upstate New York. Dad drinks gin and tonics with Grandma, and I drink virgin margaritas with Grandpa, and after a week, we're set with money for another year. It usually involves me having to perform on the piano (ugh) or sing (double ugh), but by that time we've all had enough to eat and drink that no one cares.

Listen, I'm not endorsing this as a lifestyle. But it's nice work if you can get it.

I've tried at various points to use some of the money to help my mom's mom—my *shimasani*—out on the Navajo Reservation. But she refuses to take anything from me. She says she likes life just as it is.

"So why do you think the aliens haven't come out to talk yet?" I asked. "They've been on the ground for five days now. Doesn't that seem like a long time for them to just sit inside their ship?" Dad stopped typing just long enough to push his glasses up his nose, but didn't answer.

"For all we know," I went on, "they could be preparing to leave the ship and spread the alien equivalent of smallpox, or just kill us all outright."

"It's like the Mall of America all over again," he said.

"Seriously, Dad," I said. "Are these good aliens or bad aliens?"

"At this point we don't know if there are aliens on the ship at all," he answered, leaning over me to look out the window. "It could be unmanned."

"If Hollywood has taught us anything, it's that there are only two kinds of aliens: invading aliens who want to kill us all, and peaceful aliens who want to enlighten us with their wisdom. Personally, I have a hard time seeing us being receptive to either kind."

"You don't think we'd welcome a mixture of E.T. and the Dalai Lama, right after he flattened half the state?"

"Two states. I think E.T. Lama ought to wear body armor."

"There are other kinds of aliens, too," he said. "Don't you ever watch *Star Trek*? Maybe these are Ferengi, and they're here to make a buck."

"Maybe they're Klingons, and they want to fight for glory and honor."

"The Klingons became friends with the Federation, Aly," he said, leaning back in his chair. "Really, it's like you aren't interested in my job at all."

"My point," I said, with all the indignation I could muster, "is that there are a lot of ways that this could go bad. They're estimating eighteen thousand people died because of this thing. I think everyone's ready for a fight."

"So now you're more worried about angry humans than evil aliens?"

"I'm just saying that this isn't going to go well, no matter what they came here for."

He patted my leg and turned back to his spreadsheet. "The National Guard is already on-site. I imagine they have their guns pointed in both directions."

"That's not very comforting."

A few hours later, the captain announced that we had started our descent. I switched off my iPhone and stared out the window. The ship itself wasn't visible from the plane as we came in to land, but the giant scar it had left across the land certainly was.

I wondered how cold it was going to be when we got out. Miami had been a delightful seventy degrees when we left. I'm not one to crave heat by any means, but I've always heard horror stories about Minnesota winters. I am not built for that kind of freeze. I figured if I couldn't be in Miami, the only kind of winter my body would accept was the kind of winter that we experienced with *Shimasani* on the reservation. The kind where you wake up to an inch of snow that's gone by afternoon. But I knew that was wishful thinking. Minnesota was not New Mexico. It was October now, and even though there were no visible signs of winter, I just knew that I was about to enter an arctic blast chiller.

My dad's job was turning my life upside down, and since a UFO crash was pretty much the biggest news to have happened in the history of history, I had a hunch we were going to be in Minnesota for a very long time. Would I spend the rest of high school here? At a boarding school?

I know that my dad had enrolled me in Minnetonka because he was going to be working twenty-four hours a day, but I wished he'd had enough faith in me to let me take care of myself. I'd have Bluebell, and I'd have credit cards, and Minnesota had to have Chinese delivery. I didn't need to be shipped off to some preppy boarding school.

The plane was nearing the ground, and the speed of the descent seemed to amplify my anger.

"Dad, you do realize that I'm seventeen years old, right? I

should have some sort of say in my life."

"You're following me to the most amazing jobsite ever, and you're going to a school that produces the best and brightest minds in this country. Did you know that John F. Kennedy went to this school? Margaret Thatcher? Martin Luther nailed his Ninety-five Theses to the front door."

"You made all of that up."

"Maybe I did," he said, and closed his laptop as the plane touched ground. "And maybe I didn't. You'll never know."

"I'll know as soon as I turn my phone back on."

"And by then I'll be safely off the plane and running for the car."

"If I'm coming to this school just to be near you and the crash site, then you'd darn well better take me to see the ship first."

"Right now it's surrounded by army men with guns that shoot real bullets. So probably not today, but soon. And don't worry. The ship is half a mile tall and three miles long. You'll get a good view of it, no matter where we are."

When we got inside the completely empty airport, I made Dad stop at the Starbucks, where I got a caramel latte, expecting I'd need it in the face of the freezing temperatures outside. Starbucks was the only business open in the entire airport—even the people movers were turned off.

We headed for the rental car counters. Dad got a new sedan—a Toyota something or other—and handed me the keys. It was against the rules—you have to be at least twenty-one to drive a rental car—but he had a driver waiting to pick him up and take him to the crash site and I had to get to school somehow.

The whole time we were at the airport, I couldn't help being amazed that life was rolling along as much as it was, considering these people had just had a UFO crash in their front yard. The rental car agents still tried to sell us extra insurance; the Starbucks workers still smiled cheerfully. Once I found the car, I told the GPS to take me to the school, and then I changed my mind. Why shouldn't I get to see the ship for myself? So I told the GPS to find Lakeville and headed down Interstate 35. The road was completely blocked leading into town, but Dad was right—even from a distance, the ship was impossible to miss.

I had been watching near-constant coverage of the site for the past five days, but even so, seeing it in real life was amazing. It was enormously tall, especially against the background of farmland. They said on the news that it was half a mile high—so it was basically the size of two and a half Empire State Buildings. Seeing it up close, I couldn't help but feel a rush of emotion. On all the news shows, they'd had person after person tell stories about how they'd been in their house and decided to go to the grocery store a mile or two down the road—they'd been safe, but the rest of their family had died. And here was the thing that had done the damage, the killing.

I pulled out my phone and took a bunch of pictures to send to my friends back home. They could find better photos online and on TV—there were camera crews everywhere—but this was proof that I was really here, right in the middle of it. Proof that I was actually gone for good.

I took one last picture: the front of the ship had plowed up a mountain of dirt, and the mound was just touching a little red-and-white farmhouse. The luckiest people in Minnesota.

I got back in my car and told the GPS to take me to the "Minnetonka School for the Gifted and Talented." A line pointed off away from all the action and toward my new life.

Well, by way of a mall. I needed some freaking sweaters and a parka.

TWO

It was nearly dark by the time I pulled up at the school's wrought iron front gate. There was an electronic buzzer and speaker, and I leaned out of my window to press the button.

A tinny male voice answered. "Can I help you?"

"Alice Goodwin," I said. "I'm new."

There was a long pause, long enough that I thought I might need to press the button again, but the tinny voice came back eventually. "We expected you earlier."

"It's been a heck of a day," I said. "As you can probably imagine. My dad's with NASA."

"Yes, yes," the voice replied, in a tone that indicated he couldn't care less that aliens had landed five days before. "Drive through the gate and come up to the parking lot on the south side of the building. We'll send someone to meet you."

The wrought iron gate slid noiselessly open in front of me, and I drove up a hill to the school. As the road curved around the back, I could see the difference between the new portion and the old portion of the building—the front was stone and brick and looked old, but the back two-thirds appeared to be less than five years old. The exterior walls were mostly glass, and I saw students milling around inside. No one seemed to notice my car pull into the parking lot. Not that I expected everyone to drop what they were doing and race down to meet the new girl. But a few casual glances would have been more welcoming.

The parking lot was what I was expecting. Six Mercedes, four Audis, two Lexuses, three Porsches, and five BMWs. There was also the odd Honda and Chevy thrown into the mix, just to spice things up. I pulled my rented Toyota into a spot between two Mercedes and wondered what it would be like going to a school where so many people had so much money.

A shortish guy with jet-black hair, olive skin, and rectangular glasses came walking down the steps just as I was trying to carry my luggage and all my shopping bags up into the building.

"Hey," I said, fumbling with the three boxes of shoes. "A little help?"

He hurried over and grabbed the majority of the stuff from me. "You're a newbie?"

He was wearing the uniform, or the evening-casual version of it. Khaki pants, a white oxford shirt, a loosened tie. I tried to put on an air of confidence, as though I started at new schools all the time and this was nothing special.

"Yep," I said. "Alice Goodwin. Take me to your leader."

He didn't respond.

"UFO joke," I said, and moved past him toward the door. He was cute, and I was making a great impression.

"I take it you're here because of the aliens?" he asked, and then paused. "I mean, not like you came here in the ship or anything. But are you here because they're here?"

"My dad works for NASA. How did you guess?"

"Because most other people are packing up and leaving," he said. I held the door for him and he sidled through.

"What about you? Not afraid of aliens?"

"Nowhere to go," he said. "Dad's in Abu Dhabi. Mom's in Singapore. Business must be done. I did get a text from Mom, though. Four words. 'UFO in Minnesota—crazy.' So, as you can tell, they're pretty concerned."

There was a rapid clacking on the marble floor. A moment later a woman appeared around the corner.

"Miss Goodwin," she said, a fake smile on her face. "I'm Mrs. Lund. We were expecting you much earlier."

"All's well that ends well," I said.

"I see you've met Mr. Malik."

"I see that I have," I said, turning and nodding to him. "Hi, Malik."

"It's Kurt," he said. "Kurt Malik."

"Well, Mr. Malik, since you are already holding Miss Goodwin's parcels, perhaps you'd be willing to show her to the dormitories?"

"Sure thing," he said.

"Miss Goodwin," the secretary said. "You're in room one-oh-nine. You're expected in Mrs. Cushing's office tomorrow morning at eight o'clock, sharp."

"Sharp," I said, and nodded. She turned on her heel and strode away.

"So," I said to Kurt as we walked. "You weren't sent outside to help me?"

"Guilty as charged. That was probably why Mrs. Lund came. But why should I have argued with you? A fellow human in need? We're all going to be soylent green by morning."

"I don't think aliens had anything to do with soylent green."

"Well, either way. We'll all be pod people eventually. Let's make a bet: I'll put twenty bucks on pod people."

"I'll put twenty on weird alien disease. Alien smallpox. Either way, thanks for helping me."

We moved through a large common room, where two

dozen students were clustered around a large-screen TV, and then we passed the cafeteria, where more students were watching TV.

"Has anything big happened in the last few hours?" I asked.

He laughed. "You sound less concerned about this than anyone I know."

"My dad's with NASA. For him, this is all exciting. I've never seen him so thrilled, not when we landed the rover on Mars or when they landed that thing on a comet. His enthusiasm rubs off on me, I guess. He hardly gave my blue hair a second glance." Sure, it was a lie, but I didn't expect this boy and my dad to be having serious conversations about my hair color any time soon.

"They're going to make you dye it out," he said. "'No extreme hairstyles.'"

"One streak? This is hardly extreme," I said. "I could have gotten extreme."

He set down one armload of bags and brushed his black hair forward so that it covered his eyebrows. "They consider this extreme. I've got maybe another week before I get reprimanded."

"My dad has sent me to a prison."

Kurt picked up the bags again. "It's not bad. It's just wealthy. People expect a certain amount of grooming when they're wealthy."

He turned a corner and came to a door that was very sparsely decorated with Halloween paraphernalia—a single small ghost hung in the center of the door, and a construction-paper sign labeled it as "Ghouls" instead of Girls.

"I'm a Ghoul, huh?"

"Better than us," he said. "We got 'Mensters.'"

"Seriously?"

"Seriously. Anyway, this is as far as I can take you. Wealth also means respect, decorum, and dignity, and one of those words means that I'm not allowed to carry your bags to your dorm room."

"I'll manage."

"If you want to watch more coverage of the UFO not doing anything, come down to the cafeteria later. I plan to gorge myself on pie. We're all dead, so it doesn't matter, right?"

"Right."

He held the door open for me and I waddled into the girls' dorm hall. This part of the building looked very new and very sterile.

The doors were decorated off and on with Halloween decor. Room 109 was at the end of the first hall, just before a turn that led deeper into the dorm. It had a cartoon of a sexy devil and a sign announcing the inhabitants of the room to be succubi.

I knocked and tried to put on my best succubus look,

although I assumed it looked very similar to my haggard *I've spent all day traveling and shopping* look.

The door opened, and someone came out who looked even less like a succubus than I did—she was tall and willowy, dressed in a gray sweatshirt and flannel pajama pants. Her red hair was pulled back in a frizzy ponytail.

"Hi!" she exclaimed. "You're the new girl!"

"I'm the new girl," I agreed. "You're the succubus?"

She gestured up and down her body. "A demon who seduces men," she said with a laugh. "And then kills them. That's me all right." She reached out to take some of my bags. "Been shopping? What did you get?"

"Sweaters," I said. "It's cold here."

"You're from Florida, right? I'm so sorry." She led me inside to a surprisingly large common room with four desks and two couches. Through doors to each side I saw bedrooms with two beds each. Everything looked new, and clean, and like I would be totally miserable. I'd never shared a room in my life, ever.

"I assume you're used to this weather?"

"No," she said, setting my bags on one of the beds. "By which I mean 'hell no.' I'm from Atlanta. You can't tell from my accent?"

She didn't have the slightest twinge of a southern accent, and as I opened my mouth hesitantly to say something, she laughed and sat down. "Don't worry. I'm technically from

Atlanta, but I never lived there long enough for it to matter. Elementary at St. Barbara's School for Girls in Pasadena. Junior high at St. Rose in Santa Fe."

"No saints for you anymore? Hence the succubus?"

She opened one of my shoeboxes and pulled out the black leather pair, and immediately measured the heel with her fingers.

"The succubus thing is Brynne's. I'm Rachel, by the way. They'll never let you wear these shoes. The heel is too high."

I sighed and dropped my bags onto the bed. "It's hardly an inch and a half."

"Closer to two," she said. "Besides, one inch is the limit. I just wear flats."

"One inch is hardly a shoe at all."

She grinned and opened the next box. She seemed to have no sense of my privacy. Was this what sharing rooms was going to be like? I mean, I like to pry into people's lives as much as anyone, but what is roommate etiquette?

I pointed at the box. "Those will be too tall as well, then."

"Yep," she said. "But you'll look good around the dorm." She held the shoe up to her foot. "I bet we could share."

"Be my guest. So, you and Brynne and who's in the fourth bed?"

"It was Nikki, but her parents pulled her out of here yesterday morning. People are dropping like flies. What about you? I heard you're here because of the thing."

"My dad works for NASA."

"So why aren't you staying with him?"

"Because I have a hunch he'll be living in a trailer filled with coffee cups," I said. "He gets a little passionate about his work. Even when there weren't aliens to worry about, he never got home before eight."

Rachel pulled on one of my new shoes and stood up to look in the floor-length mirror on the closet door.

"They really make the flannel pop," I said.

She turned and stuck out her tongue.

"So which are you?" I asked, still too intimidated to tackle the task of unpacking. "Gifted or talented?"

She screwed up her face into a grimace. "Honestly?"

"No, lie to me," I said. "Yes, of course, honestly."

Rachel laughed and sat down to take off the shoe. "Both. Gifted, mostly at math and science. And talented at the cello. I play a passable violin if I'm forced to."

"Are people forcing you to play a lot of violin? Is this that kind of school?"

"Not here," she said and put the shoes away, setting the box on her lap and closing the lid. "My parents think the violin is a much more appropriate instrument. Don't ask me why."

"You don't like it?"

"I'm just not as good at it," she said with a shrug. "I think it's too—I don't know—squeally? That's not even a word. But the cello is great."

"Well, the good news is that the War of the Worlds has started, so no need to worry about that now."

Rachel's face went ashen. "Is that what your dad says?"

I reached out and touched her hand. "No. I'm just kidding."

"Everyone is kidding about it," she said, her demeanor entirely changed. She picked up my bags and started hauling them into one of the bedrooms—it looked like I was sharing with her. Our names were on the doors. "The world as we know it is over and everyone is acting like it's hilarious. You know why I'm hiding out in here? Because I can't watch TV anymore. I can barely stand to be online"—she gestured toward her laptop—"because even websites that have nothing to do with the news are showing a black ribbon to honor the deaths of everyone in the path of the ship, or they're filled with essays about 'Where They Were,' or 'What This Means.' It's awful."

"Sorry," I said. It didn't seem like a good enough response, but I didn't know what else to say. I joked about aliens because it was better than freaking out. Rachel had decided to take the latter approach, and I couldn't blame her.

"It's okay," she said. "I'm not one of the people who think the world is ending. Just one who can't take the stress of everything changing. This is like the Gutenberg Bible times a million."

I smiled, and then so did she.

"That doesn't make much sense, does it?" she said.

"I get your point." I dug through one of the bags to find a pair of socks. "Do you know Kurt Malik?"

"Sure. Why?"

"I told him I'd meet him in the cafeteria to watch TV."

"Seriously?" She flopped back on the bed.

"What's wrong?"

"Do you know how often I have plans to meet guys in the cafeteria? Never. You show up and have a date before you even get to your room."

"It's not a date."

"You know what I mean. It's a thing. You have a thing with Kurt Malik."

"Do you like Kurt?"

"No, I don't like Kurt. He's not even in my top ten. But still."

"But still," I agreed. "Well, how about this: I don't really want to watch TV either. So what if I go get us both some pie or something, and I come back here and you help me unpack?"

"No," she said, sitting up. "I don't want to ruin your thing with Kurt."

"I'll cancel. If he likes me, then it'll be playing hard to get. And if he doesn't like me, then it'll be doing us both a favor."

Rachel smiled slowly. "I like the way you think. But still. What if it's your only 'thing'? I don't get a lot of things."

"There's plenty of time for more things. Tell me this, though. Do you really have a top ten list?"

"Oh, definitely. Like I said, gifted in math and science. Meaning: total dork. I have a spreadsheet."

I laughed. "And who's at the top?"

Rachel grinned. "It's a personal spreadsheet. Password protected. If I ever let it get out, then Brynne would be my worst nightmare."

Huh. I didn't want a roommate who would ever be anyone's worst nightmare. "How's that? Gossip?"

"No, not gossip. Because she'd harangue me every minute of the day to actually do something about the spreadsheet."

"So, can I take it the reason you don't have 'things' in the cafeteria with boys is because you don't ask a lot of boys to get pie with you?"

"Well, one of the girls in here put 'succubi' on the door and one of them didn't. And she meant it."

"I hate to ask it," I said, "but how exactly is Brynne gifted and talented? Or would that be a question better posed to the boys?"

"Well, she is a genius. She's just a genius in lots of ways. Unlike me. I mean, I could tutor just about every one of those guys in math—and have—but none of them remember that when Saturday night rolls around."

"Do you ever ask them?"

"I grew up inside boarding schools. They don't really teach you how to talk to boys. The only parenting I got was from guidance counselors and report cards."

"Then I guess I'll have to be your mom while I'm here."

"Thanks." She laughed, and then added in a bratty little kid voice, "You told me you were going to get me pie, Mom."

THREE

The selection of pie was actually pretty good. In fact, the selection of everything was pretty good. Rachel told me classes had been canceled and most of the students had spent the day in one of the many common rooms, while the cafeteria churned out meal after meal, dessert after dessert. The UFO landing was going to be the single leading cause of heart disease at the Minnetonka School for the Gifted and Talented.

Kurt was there, sprawled out on a sofa with no room for me to sit beside him. He saw me walk in and hopped over the back of the couch to trot after me. I broke the news to him that I was going back to the dorm rather than staying with him, and he didn't seem too heartbroken, which threw me for a loop. Wasn't he supposed to be devastated? Instead

I got, "That's cool," as he helped himself to more banana cream.

"Any exciting new developments?" I asked, balancing four slices of pie—two cherry, one key lime, and one coconut crème—on two plates. I wondered how I was going to open the dorm door.

"They've had to call in more military to get a better perimeter around the ship because protestors keep trying to get over to it."

"Why?"

"I don't know. But some guy made it all the way to the ship and started attacking it with a crowbar," he said. "They've been playing that video a lot. You should have seen them take the guy down. A beautiful chop block. The military says they're going to shoot anyone who tries to get in, because they're worried about bombs."

"Wow. Well, welcome to Earth."

"I can't say I blame the people protesting," Kurt said. "They keep saying that the death toll is going to rise—right now they're still at eighteen thousand, but three thousand more are still missing."

"Maybe I should stop being so flippant."

He shrugged. "People deal with stuff in different ways. Some people make jokes and some people attack things with crowbars."

He grabbed one of the forks I was holding and helped

himself to a bite of the coconut crème, then licked some extra cream off the fork.

"Hey," I said, awkwardly trying to pick up a second fork without dropping my plates.

Another guy came over to the pie table and pointed to my hair while he cut a slice of cherry. "Nice blue. They'll make you dye it."

"We'll see how long I can hold out," I said. "I figure I'm in the clear at least as long as classes are canceled."

"For being new, you're already pretty eager to break the rules. I like that." He put his hand to his chest. "I'm William."

"I'd shake your hand if I wasn't carrying pie," I said. "Nice to meet you, William. Can I call you Will?"

His eyes narrowed into tired, annoyed slits. "No. Just William. Anyway, classes are probably going to be out again tomorrow. And maybe Friday, if we can milk it."

Kurt looked at me. "So I'm betting you can keep the hair until Monday."

"Tuesday," I said, with a smile. "Anyway, I have to take this back to Rachel."

"Redhead Rachel?" William asked.

"Yes," I said, suddenly defensive. "She's my new roommate."

He lowered his voice. "You're new here, so I'll help you out. Rachel is trying everything she can to beat me for the Bruner in math. But it isn't going to happen. I mean look at her—frizzy hair and never wears any makeup. Introvert. Half of the award is citizenship. Leadership. You know, like proving that you will represent the school well. And Rachel's got a screw loose."

"You're kidding, right?" I didn't know what the Bruner was, but if I was going to choose someone to represent me, it wouldn't be William.

A short girl with platinum blond hair in a pixie cut and thick eyeliner appeared next to me. "Hi, I'm Brynne," she said. "Your other new roomie." She glared at William. "So, Will, how does that hazing charge get you good citizenship? I know your parents got it covered up, but it would be so easy to uncover it."

His face twitched, but only for an instant. "I don't know what you're talking about." He looked like a snake, ready to bite if provoked.

"Hazing?" I said. "That's more than just losing a scholarship. That's criminal and civil lawsuits. I bet your parents would love that." I liked provoking snakes. He took a step toward me, and I held my ground.

"Hey, Alice," Brynne said, tugging on my sleeve. "Let's get back to the room."

"Okay," I said, my eyes still fixed on his. "See you, Will. You seem fun."

Brynne grabbed one of my plates of pie, and we headed to the dorm.

"So you're the succubus?" I asked.

"We all are," she said. "The whole room."

"You're not fleeing? Heading home because aliens have landed?"

"I'm here on scholarship. Flying home at a moment's notice isn't part of the deal."

"Really?" I asked, eying her perfect hair, perfect body, and immaculate clothes. "You look so, well, money."

"Good genes," she said. "Which is actually how I ended up here. Good genes. I won the national science fair last year."

"Like *won* won? The whole thing?"

"Yep. Genetics. I thought about taking a bunch of tests during the summer to skip the rest of high school and go straight to college, but Minnetonka made me an offer I couldn't refuse. I get to do research instead of going to most of my classes, I have a full ride, and when I graduate from here I can practically write my own ticket to wherever I want. Maybe I'll already be published. That's the plan anyway. Not bad for a girl from Nowhere, Kansas."

I nodded. "Gifted and talented."

"That's what they say."

"I'm here because my dad works for NASA," I said, feeling stupid about it. "So it's not my gifts or talents—it's his."

"I'm sure that's not true," Brynne said. "We'll figure out your G and Ts." She opened the door to our room and

Rachel looked up from where she was lying on the couch, reading *David Copperfield.*

"Here," I said. "One cream, one fruit. I didn't know which you would want."

Brynne opened one of my shoe boxes. "Alice had the pleasure of meeting the wonderful William. He was as charming as always."

I grimaced. "What is his deal? Please tell me he's just here because his family paid his way in."

Brynne laughed. "Nope. William is definitely in the gifted category. He's vying for the top math scholar spot. Ooh. These are cute."

Rachel took a forkful of whipped cream. "You'll find that every room in this school is named after someone."

Brynne smirked. "One day I'm going to come back and donate. The Brynne Fuller Memorial Janitor's Closet. It's the only room left, I think."

"They'll start putting plaques on the dorms," Rachel said. "Brynne Fuller Made Out with Mark Richardson in This Room."

"And Then Donated a Hundred Thousand Dollars," Brynne said, closing the shoe box and sitting on my bed.

"Anyway," Rachel said, reaching for one of my shopping bags. "Weren't we going to help you unpack?"

The process didn't take long. We all tried on the shoes, and Rachel fell in love with one of the sweaters. I told her she could have it, but she insisted she'd go buy one of her own. I found out that Rachel was Brynne's sugar mama—Brynne got all her stunning clothes from shopping trips with Rachel. In exchange, Brynne tutored Rachel in biology and genetics.

I tried not to feel completely out of my depth in the room. I was there with two of the front runners for Bruner Scholars, one in math and the other in biology, while I was proud that I had my social security number memorized.

Oh well. Maybe I could be the Bruner Scholar in Fast Cars and Accessorizing.

The next morning at 8:04 sharp, I was in the office of the headmistress, Mrs. Cushing, sitting in the chair opposite her and getting an austere, if nervous, lecture about the history of the school. She seemed to be eager to name drop, as though she thought I was a spy from the Large Donation Society who was checking to make sure that philanthropists were getting the appreciation they deserved: the James Moore Center for Leadership, the Lynda Day Multimedia Lab, the Jack Montague Lecture Hall. I tried to put on a serious face and do some rigorous nodding at the importance of these names.

But in the end, aliens had landed, and I could tell her heart wasn't in it. She wanted to hear from me more than I wanted to hear from her, so I relayed everything my dad had told me (which, by now, was all on the news anyway), and she listened with rapt attention.

She took down my sizes and told me that I'd have uniforms ready the next day, and in the meantime I could wear anything that fit within a small encyclopedia's worth of guidelines. From a cursory glance, it ruled out just about everything except for the uniform and perhaps Elizabethan ball gowns.

Oh, and I had to dye the blue out of my hair. I told her I would as soon as I could, and I decided that I could wait through at least four or five more warnings.

I made my way back upstairs and sat down in the cafeteria with a plate of eggs and potatoes. And I know what you're thinking: eggs and potatoes from a school cafeteria are usually powdered and frozen. But I'd swear these eggs had been hand-delivered from organic farms in the south of France, and the potatoes were yellow and purple and every color but brown. Everything tasted amazing. It made me think about my dad and the nothing he was probably eating.

I called him. The phone rang five times and went to voicemail. As I was leaving a message about the wonders of my breakfast, Kurt sat down across from me. He looked exactly the same as he had the night before, right down to the untucked shirt and loosened tie. Maybe this was just what he wore all the time. I'd have to consult my encyclopedia, but I thought it was against code.

"Good morning," he said, reaching for the pepper.

"Aren't you a little late for breakfast?" After my orientation with Mrs. Cushing, it was nearly ten o'clock.

"Maybe I was waiting for you."

"Were you? Because that would be weird."

"Would it?"

"Yes. Because you could have eaten already, and then waited for me, and still sat at this table and you wouldn't have been hungry all morning."

"But then I wouldn't have a good excuse."

I speared a potato and popped it into my mouth. "Do you need an excuse?"

"I don't know. Do I?"

"This is a very weird conversation."

"I agree," he said, now taking the salt to his food. "Because most people make up reasons for doing things. Most people would find it weird for me to wait around for you and sit down without a plate of food. But food brings people together. We're sharing a common experience, and that leads to emotional bonding."

"Let me guess," I said. "Gifted and talented: psychology."

"Gifted and talented: money."

I held up my hand. "That's me, too. High five."

Kurt slapped my hand, and then returned to his breakfast. "You're lucky. You're sharing a room with two Bruner Scholars. I share a room with three other guys who have rich, detached parents. We play a lot of video games."

My phone buzzed, and I looked down at it.

"Important business meeting?" Kurt asked.

"Message from my dad."

I clicked on it.

Turn on your TV.

I glanced up at the TV on the wall across the room. It was still on nonstop CNN. I reached for Kurt's hand and pulled him with me toward the small group of kids clustered around it.

CNN was showing the same thing they'd been showing for days—a wide shot of the ship with an inset of a commentator talking. Standard CNN format for everything.

Then the camera shifted and I saw Wolf Blitzer turning in his seat and putting his finger to his ear. The shot of him was quickly replaced with a close-up on one of the rectangular insets on the hull of the ship. It looked like any of the thousand other nooks and crannies on the side of the ship, except for the fact that it was glowing and sparking.

"What the hell is that?" someone asked, and then everyone started talking, pointing at the rectangle, calling it a door or a window or an airlock or a dozen other things. I texted my dad the same question, but I didn't get any response and I knew that I wouldn't, probably for a long time.

I sat down on the couch and felt Kurt's hand on my shoulder. I thought about shoving it off, but somehow my hand ended up in his, holding on tight. I looked down the row of

TV watchers and saw Brynne at the far end, sitting cross-legged on the floor. Some boy was absentmindedly combing through her hair with his fingers.

"Brynne," I called, "do you have Rachel's number?"

Brynne stared at me for a moment, then pulled out her phone and typed out a message.

It was like we were watching the moon landing from the point of view of moon men, waiting to see what came out of that *Apollo* landing craft.

"They don't have power," William said from across the room, a smile on his face. "They can't open their own doors. They have to cut them."

"They have power," Kurt answered. "Enough power to cut through that metal—the metal that dragged across two states without breaking."

It took a long minute for someone to find the remote, but once a girl extracted it from the couch cushions, we turned up the volume. Wolf Blitzer was talking, describing the scene. He wasn't saying anything that the rest of us weren't already thinking. No brilliant insights, just the typical news anchor babble.

A different camera angle showed us that this rectangle was higher than the tallest tree, maybe a hundred feet from the ground.

Rachel came running in, wearing flannel pajamas and a thick bathrobe. I motioned for her to sit at my feet, and once she did, I let go of Kurt's hand and put my hands on Rachel's shoulders.

"What did I miss?" she asked breathlessly.

"They're cutting their way out," a dozen people said at once. The caption at the bottom of the CNN screen read, Are They Cutting Their Way Out? Nice work, CNN.

The sparks reached the top of the rectangle and began moving across it.

An inset camera showed a group of two or three hundred soldiers advancing into the space below the rectangle.

There were alien letters written above the rectangle. Blocky and angular, and exactly the kind of font you'd expect an alien to use.

"Anybody good with languages?" I asked.

Brynne pointed to a girl. "Emily's amazing. Going to be the Bruner Scholar in languages, I bet."

Emily shrugged as she looked at the letters. "There's only a dozen letters there, if they even are letters and not numbers. Either way, that's not nearly enough to make an educated guess."

"Look at the angle," Rachel said, changing the subject. "When it breaks loose, that thing is just going to fall out. I hope whoever's inside is tethered in."

"You're hoping the aliens are okay?" another girl said with a sneer.

"Sure I am," Rachel said.

I spoke up in her defense. "If they're nice aliens, then we don't want them to get hurt. And if they're bad aliens, we don't want them to get pissed off."

"Besides," Brynne said, "way to make first contact. Whoops! Fall to your death!"

"How are they going to get down?" someone else asked.

"Helicopters," a girl said. "There are a bunch of them hovering over the ship."

Kurt leaned forward on the couch behind me. "What if it's like the Blob?" he asked. "That was an alien. What if some jelly monster comes oozing out of the hole?"

"I don't think a blob could build a ship that intricate," Brynne answered.

"And I don't think a blob could hold a blowtorch," I said. "Do we have any scale on that door? Are these things people-sized or monster-sized?"

I started braiding Rachel's hair, because I needed something to do with my hands. It was a good thing it was her sitting in front of me and not Kurt. "If they have big gray heads and big black eyes, we're going to owe the conspiracy theorists an apology."

"We already do," a guy said. "Maybe not flying saucers, but the conspiracies were right on this one."

I shook my head. "They're only right if these aliens match the theories—if they make crop circles or mutilate cattle or something. But yeah, if we get inside that ship and find big cattle mutilation factories, then I'll agree."

"No," the guy said, and he pulled out his phone. "I looked it up yesterday. The two most commonly mentioned kinds of UFO are flying saucers and 'cigar-shaped' UFOs. What is this if not cigar-shaped?"

He held his phone out to me and there was a shaky YouTube video of a gray cylinder.

"Okay," I said. "So let's say that these aliens have been coming across the galaxy for years and have been abducting our farmers and probing our backsides. Then what's the deal with this one? Did it try to scoop up an Iowan and just drop too low? Were they playing chicken with a cornfield? Was this the new guy's chance to pilot the ship and he colossally screwed up?"

The cutting torch—if that's what it was, and that's certainly what it seemed to be—had moved on to the final side of the door. This was the moment of truth.

"I think that might be it," Kurt said. "How often are you on a flight and they have a delay because of a mechanical problem? Only in this scenario, they've just flown all the way from Alpha Centauri and there's nowhere to land. Wouldn't you aim for somewhere nice and flat, like Iowa, and try not to crash?"

"Like the Sea of Tranquility," Rachel said, turning her head and almost yanking the strands of hair out of my hands. She must have noticed my blank look. "Sorry. That's where we landed on the moon—in the flattest, emptiest place we could find, so that nothing would go wrong."

They were halfway through the last side of the door. "Well," I said, "something went wrong this time."

"What if it didn't?" Rachel said, looking back at CNN. "What if this is the best possible outcome?"

"Eighteen thousand people died," a girl said.

"What if there are more than that on the ship? It's three miles long and half a mile wide. If you assume that each person has a cube ten feet by ten feet—and that's pretty generous given what things like submarines are like—you'd get a total of a hundred and thirty thousand people on there."

"Why would you call them 'people'?" the girl said with a sneer. I decided I didn't like her. She was wearing sunglasses in her hair, inside the school, in Minnesota, before lunch.

"Sorry!" Rachel said. "I should have called them aliens. I should have called them freaks. Or monsters or whatever else."

"The point still stands," Kurt said. "If there were a hundred and thirty thousand aliens in there and they were going to crash—"

"Then they should have crashed in Nevada," William said. "Or Canada, or someplace without so many people."

"Guys, look," Brynne said, and pointed. The sparking light had gone all the way around the rectangle and was back in its starting position.

Everyone was glued to the TV. The boy at the end of the couch had stopped playing with Brynne's hair, and I'd long since pulled the braids back out of Rachel's. I could smell Kurt's aftershave behind me, could see Sunglasses Girl leaning forward, elbows on knees.

The shot was a close-up of the rectangle, taken from the left side. It was zoomed in so close that the camera shook a little. But as we stared, I realized that the movement wasn't just a jiggling camera—the rectangle was moving slightly. A slight jolt at first, and then a shudder.

I got a sudden lump in my throat. This was the biggest thing that had happened in history, and I was surrounded by strangers. I needed human connection. I needed someone I cared about and who cared about me.

I took Rachel's hand, and she squeezed back.

And then the door fell away.

FOUR

The shape in the doorway was strapped into a harness. It held what looked like a large sledgehammer in its hand. Everyone in the room gasped, and Rachel and I fought to see who could break the other's fingers.

The shape, to put it simply, was human. Two legs, two arms, short hair that was as platinum blond as Brynne's, and an albino complexion. It was covered with what looked like mummy bandages everywhere but its face, hands, and feet.

The man—at least it looked like a man—hung there in the shadow of the ship, staring out at the people below.

Wolf Blitzer was giving a speech that was obviously rehearsed—someone had probably been writing it since the ship landed. CNN clearly wanted this to go down in history as one of the greatest moments on TV, and undoubtedly it would, but it felt completely manufactured.

In the darkness behind the man, I could see more shapes—different shapes. They might have looked like people, too, like humans, but it was hard to tell with the poor light and the shaking camera.

"What were you saying about them not being people?" Brynne asked, breaking the silence in the room.

"But how can they be people?" Kurt asked.

"Aliens look like people all the time," someone else said. "I mean, in movies."

"Maybe it's an alien taking a human form," William said. "Like in *GalaxyQuest*. Those aliens were really octopus things."

"Maybe it's an android," Sunglasses Girl said. "Like in that book."

"Maybe it's really just human-looking," Brynne said. "Evolution could have produced similar species on two different planets. The fact that we look the way we do allows us to have opposable thumbs, decent-sized brains, walking upright."

Rachel nodded. "And maybe it's not that big of a coincidence. Maybe these aliens sought out a world that was like their world. We're always looking for Earthlike planets. Maybe they were, too. Maybe they were looking for a species that looks like them."

"Or maybe," the conspiracy theory guy said, "they've

visited Earth before. Maybe they look like humans because they have human DNA."

We watched the TV as the alien was hauled back into the spaceship. The screen left an inset image of the opened door and then had a wider shot of the helicopters that were hovering near the door. There was no way for the helicopters to get right next to the opening, not with the curve of the ship—their rotors would hit the hull.

"So what happens now?" Sunglasses Girl asked.

"We wait and see who comes out on a long rope," I said.

"What about a fire truck?" Kurt asked. "Or would the ladder be too short?"

I answered. "Either way, I think it's safe to say that this is not a good way to start an invasion. If they were launching one, they'd come out in force, guns blazing. Not single file on a long rope."

No one responded, and I wondered if I was being too optimistic. Maybe the aliens just needed to open a hole to get fresh air, or to see what the world was like out here. Maybe there were more holes near the ground that were ready to be opened, and the aliens would come scurrying out like ants with laser guns and we'd all be dead.

One hundred thirty thousand. That was a big number. That was a colossally big number. We didn't have a hundred and thirty thousand troops on the ground. We didn't even have that many onlookers, probably.

"They must be miserable in there," I said.

Rachel glanced halfway back at me. "What do you mean?"

"My dad said the cylinder shape is to make artificial gravity. It spins, and people walk around the inside of the cylinder. But they're not spinning now."

Rachel nodded. "So they're walking on the walls and ceilings."

"And what's going to be upside down? Toilets? Algae ponds? Arboretums? I don't know," I said. "And there's no place for a hundred and thirty thousand aliens to just sit and wait. They must be desperate to get out of there."

"Then what have they been waiting for?" Sunglasses Girl asked. "Why are they just now cutting their way out?"

"Maybe they couldn't get to the tools," Kurt suggested.

The TV camera switched back to a full shot of the door, and we saw more movement inside. A male with a snow-white beard was being lowered to the ground in the harness. He was dressed the same as the first man, in a weird wrapping of rags or bandages.

This was it. There was going to be an alien foot touching Earth dirt, and even though he looked perfectly harmless, I couldn't help but think that this was all wrong and that he needed to be reeled back into the ship, and the ship needed to take off and fly into the stars, and then we could all pretend that none of this had ever happened.

But he didn't stop descending. In fact, he was moving

faster, and now someone else was following on another rope—just as wrinkled as the man, but with short white hair and the obvious curves of a human woman.

The camera changed again to show a group of people waiting below, staring up at the mummified aliens. There were five of them, two men in military uniform, one woman in a business suit, one bald man with a paunch, and the vice president.

I wondered why they'd send the vice president, when no one liked him. It must be because he was expendable, and no one knew if these aliens were going to come out and start killing everyone. Or spreading plagues.

"Hey," I said, "why is no one wearing breathing masks? Have we learned nothing from 1492?"

Brynne glanced over. "They breathe our air. That's interesting."

"Like I said," Rachel said. "Maybe they've been looking for a planet just like ours. Maybe their own planet was destroyed or something."

William rolled his eyes. "Or maybe they're here on purpose to spread germs. Look at them—they're dressed like hospital patients."

I didn't know what kind of hospitals he'd been visiting, but unless they were in ancient Egypt, he was full of crap.

The woman was descending faster than the man, and she passed him as she traveled the ten stories to the ground.

Wolf Blitzer was using the word *momentous* a lot. Momentous occasion. Momentous events. Momentous news. It was all very momentous.

I looked behind us and saw the crowd had grown to nearly forty people, including the teachers, cafeteria staff, and the janitor. Everyone wanted to see this. Everyone had to be able to say, "I remember where I was when the aliens touched the ground."

And I'd say, "I was on a couch, holding the hand of a girl I barely knew, in a town I didn't know, surrounded by people who weren't my family." But somehow, in a totally cheesy way, it made me feel bonded to the people around me. I was holding Rachel's hand as if she were my best friend in the whole world. Which maybe she was. None of my friends from my old school had called me since I left. Then again, I hadn't called any of them, either.

The camera zoomed out to show row upon row of soldiers, their guns trained on the aliens as they descended. The woman landed with an ungraceful thump, hitting the ground hard on her heels and falling on her butt. The man landed a moment later, correcting the other way and stumbling forward onto his hands and knees. The cameras zoomed in closer, giving us a better view of their pale, ghostly skin, which was barely darker than the white bandages wrapped around their bodies.

The man and woman slowly stood up, looking repulsed

by the dirt and shaking the filth from their clothing. They began to brush at each other—the man indecorously swatting at the woman's bottom. The room chuckled uncomfortably.

"A generation ship," Rachel murmured, and then turned to me. "Maybe it's a generation ship. Maybe they haven't ever seen dirt before."

"What's a generation ship?" William asked, a little disdain in his voice as he stared at the scene.

"It's when you know it's going to take longer than a lifetime to get somewhere—it's going to take generations—so people grow up and have babies and live and die all on the ship, and it's a whole new group of people who get to the planet. Maybe these people have never been off the ship."

The group of five diplomats—if that's what they were—began walking forward to meet the aliens. The vice president was in the front, and I noticed he was wearing gloves as he stretched out his hand.

There was the typical *I don't know how to shake hands* stuff that you see in every single alien movie ever, and there was a lot of talking back and forth, but no one seemed to understand each other. The vice president placed a hand on his chest and did something with his hand on his head, almost like he was indicating he wore a crown, but that couldn't be right. Or maybe it was. Maybe it was easier to signal *king* than *democracy.* Then again, who's to say that alien janitors didn't wear crowns and their kings didn't all carry mop scepters.

Interstellar communication at its finest.

Still, it was apparent from the communication that the aliens were impressed with the dress uniforms of the military men, and the alien woman's hands moved from a dangling award on one of their chests to the dangling tie around the vice president's neck and back again. Then she noticed that the man in the back had the same kind of tie, only his was striped instead of silver, and that seemed to impress her even more. The alien man was the first to approach the woman in the business suit, and he pointed to the tiny flag pin on her lapel, and then at the many pins on the military uniforms, then the men's ties, and he gave her an encouraging *Try harder next time* smile.

And then it was all gestures up to the ship above them, and the harnesses were being pulled back up, and the aliens seemed to be gesturing very quickly. The vice president was holding his hands out plaintively, and it was clear that no one was understanding anyone.

"Any lip readers in the room?" Sunglasses Girl asked.

A boy said, "It looks like he's saying, 'Welcome to Earth.'" But I didn't think it looked like that at all. To me, it looked like he was saying, "Polygamy, polygamy, polygamy," and given what the news said about our vice president, I wouldn't be surprised if he was.

The alien man launched into what must have been a prepared presentation, because the alien woman stepped back and let him play this elaborate game of interstellar charades. First, he stretched his arms wide and pointed to the sky. Then he pointed to his ship and made a snaky motion with his right hand. After that, he put his hands to his head, like he had a headache, and then darted his fingers from his head to the heads of the five-person delegation. He reached out for the alien woman, took her hand and did the same *She has a headache* sign with her hands, and then drew lines from her head toward their heads.

"I'm no interpreter," I said, "but I'd bet five bucks that they're saying they have knowledge they're going to share."

"I hope we learn each other's languages soon," Brynne said. "I don't think we'll get a lot of astrophysics insights from a game of Guess What I'm Thinking."

The next two people down the rope looked younger. The male was enormous, built like a fullback, with broad shoulders and a broad chest and broad everything. The female was short, but beautiful. Neither of them had the wrinkled, careworn look of the older pair.

They landed and the girl fell, but the guy grabbed her harness and kept her from hitting the ground. She smiled at him. I wondered if they were a couple. Or maybe brother and sister.

The next man was carrying two large packages that looked to be about the size and weight of bowling balls, and the woman following him had two packages of her own.

Wolf Blitzer got very excited about this and a commentator—a man who had formerly worked at NASA and had written a book—was listing all the possible things that they could be holding. But we never got to see what they were, because the first four aliens now followed the delegation into a tent that had been erected nearby and the harnesses went back up into the ship, and the remaining two stood there against the cold breeze, shivering, but never unwrapping their packages.

Wolf Blitzer: "Well, that was really momentous. Truly momentous."

FIVE

Aliens continued coming down. They were all dressed in some variation of mummy bandages, and it made me worry for the future of fashion. I could imagine some designer in New York saying "Scrap everything—we're moving entirely to mummy chic!"

Not all of the aliens had white hair, but they were all fair. The darkest of them had very light reddish-blond hair.

A woman, who Kurt told me was one of the school's English teachers, said we ought to journal about our thoughts and feelings. I told Kurt that *journal* is a noun and not a verb. He told me to stop being a prescriptivist. I slugged him in the shoulder.

He offered to take me on a tour of the school, and since I was getting bored watching the aliens—think about that:

they only emerged a couple hours ago, and I was getting bored watching *aliens*—I agreed.

"How long have you gone here?" I asked as we left the common room.

"Since freshman year. But I've spent my life in boarding schools. I even have the pleasure of staying for summer semesters."

"They have summer semesters here?"

"Is this your first boarding school?" he asked. "Most of them offer summer school, because if your parents are too busy to care about you nine months out of the year, they're probably too busy to care about you twelve months out of the year."

"Sorry," I said.

"No worries. I honestly think mine just really love their jobs. They don't even see each other. I can't remember the last time my parents lived in the same city. They're both in finance, and no, I don't know what that means, except that they're rich, but they think they're poor because they're always dealing with other, richer people's money. I'm the kid who happened accidentally. You should see us on vacation: every summer for two weeks we go on a private yacht somewhere, and they spend all their time on their cell phones and laptops—we never go far enough from shore for them to lose cell reception."

"Sounds awesome."

"I like school better. I'm used to it."

"Next summer you can come visit me in Miami. We'll do normal person things."

He pointed to a door that was decorated with fake blood and the Mensters sign. "There's our dorm. No girls allowed."

"Speaking of which, how strict are they with rules around here?" I asked, walking past the door.

"Depends," he said. "They're tasked with raising us to be just as successful as our parents, so they're really strict about things like homework and testing. And if you do anything remotely illegal, you're in deep trouble. But they're lax on other things. So, for example, you can break curfew every night as long as you're getting straight A's. And girls go in the boys' dorms all the time, so long as no one is smoking or whatever else."

"'Whatever else' seems to encompass a lot."

He grinned. "You'll get a feel for it. Just remember: if it will hurt your chances of getting into college or getting elected, they're going to punish you for it."

We walked up a long set of stairs that led into the old part of the building. There was a very distinct change—they didn't try to make the transition smooth at all. It just stopped being steel and cement and became marble and oak. I felt like I was stepping back in time.

"If I were a better host I'd tell you the history of the building, about how the awards in this trophy case represent

Minnetonka's win against our rival school in the 1939 something or other, but I have no idea about any of that stuff."

I stopped at the trophy case. There was a very large brass cup with a plaque that said "First Place, Minnetonka School."

"Well, that's explanatory," I said.

He pointed at a picture. "They look like they're in football uniforms, maybe? But we don't have a football team here. We have soccer and field hockey and lacrosse."

"I'm gonna go with lacrosse," I said, and then continued down the corridor.

Kurt stopped in front of another display case. "Here's the real deal with this school. The donor wall. I mean, there's a museum on the third floor that has an amazing private collection, but this donor wall really explains Minnetonka."

I scanned the case, looking at the dozens of plaques and pictures. Friends of Minnetonka got their name on just a tiny plaque. Platinum Friends and Diamond Friends got progressively bigger nameplates. Honored Friends got photos, and every one of the pictures was of someone I recognized—business leaders who were always on the covers of magazines. Politicians. A Nobel Prize winner. And in the center of it all was a past president of the United States.

"He didn't go here," I said. "I would have heard about that from Mrs. Cushing."

"He didn't," Kurt said. "His son did."

"I feel honored?" I said. "I guess?"

"Here's my bet," he said, leaning his back against the mahogany-and-brass case and folding his arms. "The school has a waiting list a mile long. But when they got the call from your dad, they didn't see a regular rich girl, they saw a way to connect themselves to the biggest event in history. You're their ticket to all things alien."

I rolled my eyes. "Great."

"No, you don't get it: this is great for you. They're not trying to build your resume—they're using you to build *their* resume. You can get away with murder."

"Really?"

"Really."

"Then I don't think I'm going to dye this blue out of my hair."

SIX

My dad called after lunch. I was in my dorm room, scanning the internet for any interesting news that CNN wasn't reporting. When my phone buzzed I snatched it up and answered before it could vibrate twice.

"Hey, Dad."

Rachel and Brynne both looked over, knowing I was potentially going to get the information we were all looking for.

"Hey, Aly," he said. "I don't have a lot of time. How's school?"

"Shut up, Dad, and tell me about the aliens."

"Promise me you're not going to talk to reporters."

"I'm going to talk to my roommates."

"Any of them work for the *New York Times*?"

"Come on, Dad."

"Well, we've started talking to them. They have a machine that can translate languages. It's a learning machine, so the more we talk, the better it gets. It's really an amazing piece of technology."

"And what are they saying?"

"Patience, my dear. The president is going to address the nation tonight and talk about that," he said. "He's meeting with the leader of the aliens soon."

Brynne waved her hand. "Ask him why they look like humans!"

"Dad? Why do they look like humans?"

"We haven't figured that one out yet. But we were as surprised as you. They breathe our air, and the gravity in the ship seems to have been pretty equivalent to the gravity here—this is what they were used to."

"In movies aliens always look human."

"That's because it's cheaper to give a guy Spock ears or green skin than it is to make creatures that aren't humanoid. But these guys don't even have Spock ears."

"They're really pale."

"That's probably from spending so much time on the spaceship," he said. "We think they lived on the ship their whole lives."

"Like a generation ship?" I said, and Rachel's face broke into a big smile.

"No," he said. "Well, kinda. Okay, I'm just guessing here, but I think they lived on this ship permanently. I think they were on the ship long enough that the pigment in their skin evolved out, like how salamanders in caves are albinos. Granted, I'm not a biologist. I'm just—"

"You're frickin' director of special projects for NASA," I said. "And I'm going to tell the *New York Times* that you said they're salamanders."

"It still doesn't explain why they look human, though," he said thoughtfully. "As soon as we can we're going to get a DNA sample. But given how hard it's been to convince them to go along with our security measures—the fences and the guards with machine guns and numbers we've pinned to their chests—I don't know how long it'll be before they let us take their blood."

"I have to say that I'm proud of you, Dad. You didn't just lock them up like in *E.T.* You're behaving much more like *Close Encounters of the Third Kind*. Good job."

"There are people who want to tackle them and perform tests," he said. "The only reason we haven't done it is because we don't know how many of them are in that ship. People here are scared, Aly."

"They don't have weapons, do they?"

"We don't know what they have. A lot of them are carrying packages, and we don't know what's in them. The only tech that we've seen from them is that translator. And that's sufficiently advanced to make us all nervous."

"But they seem nice, don't they? I saw the game of charades where they drew lines from their brains to the vice president's brains."

"You saw that, huh? Yeah, they definitely want to tell us something. We just need to figure out what. So, how are things with you? Are you married to a doctor yet?"

"They're not doctors here," I said. "Politicians."

"Yikes," he said. "You don't have my permission to marry a politician."

"I'll try to restrain myself."

"Hey, Aly. I've got to go. But I'm going to call you back soon. I've got a job for you to do."

"Seriously?" I said with too much enthusiasm. "I mean: Okay. Call me soon."

"Love you."

"You, too."

I hung up the phone and looked up into the expectant eyes of my roommates.

"He said he had a job for me to do soon, which I'm going to translate into me and my two roommates will have a job to do soon."

I tried to relay the conversation as word for word as I could, but Dad hadn't really given me a lot of hard facts. Still, his guesses were better than most people's facts.

"That makes sense about the pigment in the skin and

hair evolving out," Brynne said. "If they were always on a ship. I wonder if it was dark on the ship, or if there just wasn't any UV light—maybe their artificial light is harmless."

Rachel nodded. "It would also explain why they seemed surprised by dirt. But still—what's the purpose of a ship if they never leave it? Do they not have a planet of their own? Are they completely self-sustaining? Do they never have to stop somewhere to pick up supplies?"

"Algae," Brynne said. "I've read about it for long space voyages. Produces oxygen, and they can live off it. They recycle their body water."

"Their pee," I said. "That sounds less gross than 'body water.'"

"But nothing is completely sustainable," Rachel said. "You don't pee out as much as you drink. Your body consumes calories that it doesn't give back. They'd have to refill on supplies somewhere."

"Maybe that's why they came here," I said. "Maybe they were passing through and saw a planet with people similar to them, and they accidentally crashed."

"It seems hard to accidentally crash something that big."

"It seems harder to fly something that big," I said.

Brynne tapped her tablet screen. "By the latest count, they've passed the four thousand mark. Aliens who have come out, I mean."

I opened my laptop back up. "Are they all still standing out in the open?"

"The army is putting up tents," Brynne said. "But I bet they're cold. Fox News has a picture of a woman alien holding a baby."

"Really? Does it look like a human baby?" Rachel asked.

"It's not a larva," I answered.

A girl popped her head in the door. "Hey, guys."

"Hey, Emily," Brynne said.

"The president is speaking tonight, now that he's had a chance to communicate with the aliens."

"That'll be weird," I said. "How much could they have communicated this fast?"

Emily moved into the doorway and leaned on the jamb. "Faster than you might think. There was a study out of the University of Utah—"

"Nerd!" Brynne called out, and threw her pillow at Emily.

Another girl appeared behind Emily—a girl dressed like one of the aliens, in mummy rags. "Today I officially say, 'Who cares?' You know what this school needs? A party. And what would a party be like without the succubi?"

It turns out that it's not that hard to throw a party if you go to the Minnetonka School. The cafeteria is always stocked with a hefty array of desserts, and there's a soda machine and chips with six different kinds of salsa. It's a wonder that everyone in this school isn't overweight. Well, not really—pretty much every student is a type A personality with an eating disorder.

Not me, though, and I made sure to force chips and pie and cheesecake onto everyone.

We were wearing our alien suits, of course. It only took Brynne trying on her skintight mummy costume (a leotard wrapped in strips of cloth from cut-up bedsheets) and parading down the hall for all the other girls to decide they needed to compete or be completely overshadowed. And somehow the boys got wind of it, and they were doing their best; there were a lot of abs, biceps, and pectorals on display. None of us looked exactly like the aliens, but we looked like their alternately sexier/shabbier versions.

Someone plugged their iPod into the TV, and we all danced as we waited for the president to speak.

I learned a lot at the party. I learned that Sunglasses Girl always wore sunglasses in her hair, even when she was dressed up as an alien. I also learned that her name was Hannah, and that her dad was a senator from South Carolina. I even learned that she knew how to dance really dirty and attracted a lot of attention from the guys. So, enlightening.

I overheard one of the dorm resident assistants asking another if we should be acting like this in the middle of a national emergency, and the other one said that everyone mourns in different ways. It hadn't occurred to me that we were even mourning—I had been so caught up in the aliens coming out of their ship that I hadn't thought much about the people in the path of the crashed spaceship. But I also got the feeling that the counselor thought we should be mourning all the time, for the sake of our waning youth, or our uncertain future, or for all the people who were outside Minnetonka and not getting to dance like aliens. Maybe he was right. Or maybe he needed to eat more habanero salsa.

The music cut out and everyone turned to look at the TV. The shot had changed to the president standing at a podium. He was in a tent by the spaceship, dressed in a suit and tie, like always. Beside him stood four of the aliens—the four who had first emerged from the ship.

"Tonight I greet not only my fellow Americans, but also the people of the world. An historic step has been taken today, and we now know beyond a shadow of a doubt that we are not alone.

"Let me begin with what we know. Six days ago, an alien craft crashed onto Earth. We now know that this crash was an accident, and I want to stress that this disaster was in no way a part of our alien visitors' plans. I have assured them that the American people will recognize this for what it was—a terrible, terrible accident. We have no intent to punish these well-intentioned people for what has happened.

"I have been in communication with them all afternoon, and soon we plan to introduce them to the United Nations, as they are visitors not just to America, but to the entire human race." He gestured to the bearded man beside him. "This is Mai, and he is the leader of this group. They call themselves the Guides. It is indeed unfortunate that they landed in such a tragic fashion as their intentions were to come here to help us as a people, to teach."

Emily, the languages expert, shouted, "That's bullshit. They came here to teach? Teach what?"

Everyone shushed her, although I was sure many people agreed.

"America welcomes the Guides. I've spent the last few hours with Mai, and I feel his group poses no threat. We will be setting up shelters for them as they are transferred out of their spacecraft and slowly integrated into society. We are taking every step to make sure that everyone is safe, both human and alien. We will be protecting everyone—everyone—from threats to their health and to their physical safety.

"For those of you who are suffering tonight, we are mobilized to help you. For those who are concerned, let me assure you: we are taking every precaution. We will constantly be updating America and the world. God bless you, and God bless America."

Maybe it was the Navajo in my blood and the history of Native American oppression, but the idea that these aliens were here to teach us didn't really work for me. I wasn't going to stubbornly insist that there was no possible way that someone might have a better idea of how things ought to be done. But these guys had just wiped out twenty thousand people. And they expected us to listen to their ways of peace and prosperity? Fine, it was an accident. We all make mistakes. But this was like someone driving a semitruck through your living room, running over your grandpa, and then getting out of the cab and telling you how to move on.

And were they really calling themselves the Guides? Could you get any more pretentious?

I suddenly wanted to be out of my stupid alien costume. I didn't want anything to do with them. I stormed out of the party, my bare feet slapping on the cold cafeteria tile. I was already yanking off strips of fabric by the time I got to the Ghouls sign, and was down to my sports bra and shorts when I got to my room, a trail of torn bedsheets in my wake.

I yanked my phone from the table and called my dad. It rang once and went to voicemail.

"What the hell, Dad? Guides? They're here to tell us what to do? Call me back, because this is ridiculous, and I need to know that the world isn't just rolling over and letting these people—these aliens—tell us how to live our lives."

I hung up and tossed the phone on the bed beside me.

After about ten minutes I got a text from him. **Swamped with work. Can you do dinner Wednesday?**

I texted back with **Sure. Love you.**

He didn't reply. He always replies. He always tells me he loves me. Damn those aliens.

There was a knock at the door.

"Come in," I shouted.

"Are you sure?" It was a male voice. "There's a lot of clothing that didn't make it to your room."

"I'm decent, Kurt," I said, leaning back against the wall. "You're not supposed to be in here."

"A lot of things aren't how they're supposed to be."

"I don't need you to be all sympathetic. I just want my dad to answer his phone."

He sat down at the empty desk and turned the chair to face me.

"So what are you thinking?" he asked after a moment.

"What do you think I'm thinking? This is bullcrap." I left him in the common room and went into the bedroom to pull on a sweater and a pair of jeans.

"I'm not even American, and I agree with you."

"You're not American?"

"Technically Indian," he said. "I've been in America since elementary school though. My first name's not Kurt. It's Karthik."

"So I learn there are alien Guides and my friend isn't American all on the same day," I said, elbowing him in the ribs as I stepped back out of the bedroom and plopped down on the couch, leaning next to him.

"I'm more American than I am anything else. I just don't have the citizenship."

"So you're not going to be a politician in the politician mill?"

"Not planning on it."

"I bet there are a lot of phone calls happening right now," I said. "I bet Hannah's calling her dad."

"And Ricky's dad is a congressman," Kurt said. "And so are Emily Fenton's and Emily Hughes's dads. The Congressional Emilys."

I pulled a throw pillow up to my chest. "This is stupid, Kurt."

"I agree. I'm amazed the president even said we'd listen to the Guides. You've got to know that his approval rating will plummet. He'll look weak and conciliatory. Maybe he's going to try to pass the problem off to the UN. That's what he ought to do."

"I was defending the aliens," I said. "All day. I was defending them. I was pissed off when Hannah said they weren't people. When others wanted to shoot first and ask questions later."

"Your dad works for NASA," Kurt said with a shrug. "Of course you'd defend the aliens."

"Honestly, this seems worse than if they landed and started a fight. This is them landing and saying that they're smarter than us and we should want to be like them. And we have to listen because we feel guilty that they just got stranded on our planet with no hope of getting back home."

"It's worse than that," he said, standing up and moving to sit next to me on the couch. "What if they *are* smarter than us? What if they have some really great ideas, and we have to change everything?"

I turned to look him in the eye. "Do you believe that?"

"I think they dress funny," he said, looking back at me.

I smiled.

"They don't look evil," I finally said, turning away from him and staring at the floor. "They look nice. They look normal."

He turned away, staring at whatever I was staring at. "They do look normal. Maybe they are? Maybe this was all just a horrible accident, like the worst kind of first impression ever, and now they'll be labeled as bad forever."

My phone rang at eleven that night, and I snatched it up, assuming it was Dad.

"Hello?"

The voice on the other end had a rich, melodic accent, but was scratchy, like a vinyl record. *"Tsosi."*

"Shimasani!" I said, and sat up in bed. My grandma didn't have a phone at home—she used the pay phone at the gas station, which meant I couldn't ever get hold of her; she had to call me.

"Ya'at'eeh."

"*Ya'at'eeh, Shimasani!* I'm so glad you called. Have you seen the news?"

"Yes, yes. Is your father working on it?"

"He is. We moved to Minnesota."

"You're sixteen now. You need to come back to the reservation."

"I'm seventeen," I said. "And I had my *kinaalda* when I was thirteen."

"But I need to see you. My daughter had only one daughter. I don't like what I'm seeing on television, on the news. I have much to teach you."

"And I want to learn it," I said, really meaning it. The peace and calm of the reservation was better than any vacation. "But right now I have to be here for Dad. He's working too hard, and he needs someone to take care of him."

"Your mother died so young."

I didn't know what to say to that, so I just went with, "Yeah."

There was a long pause.

"Are you there, *Shimasani*?"

"I'm here. Come visit me. Bring your friends."

"I will."

"Someone else needs the phone."

"I love you."

"Ayóó áníínishní."

The call disconnected.

SEVEN

I settled into the school over the next few days, getting used to the dorm and the common rooms and my roomies and Kurt without having to worry about homework getting in the way. We watched the fund-raising concert for the families of the victims. Brynne and Rachel and I just saw it on the couch in the common room, but some of the kids paid for tickets and went: the concert was playing in the Minnesota Vikings stadium. We saw Emily Fenton in the front row, getting high-fived by Taylor Swift, and we thought she'd died, the way she swooned.

The next night was much more somber. The student body president had organized a candlelight vigil, so we all put on our heavy coats and stood outside while someone sang "Amazing Grace." I thought something from *Frozen* might have been more appropriate, or even "Baby, It's Cold Outside." But instead of taking requests, we had the world's longest moment of silence, and yes, I'm a baby, and yes, I'm probably going to hell for thinking about hypothermia during the silent moment instead of the many people who died.

I ended that night sipping from a large mug of hot chocolate while sitting by the fireplace in the common room, leaning against Kurt. For warmth, that's all. Seriously, that's how people warm up. Read any survival handbook.

Anyway, all good things must come to an end, and on Monday, classes resumed and I found myself in AP U.S. History. AP U.S. History is the same no matter where you go, I discovered. I'd been there for twenty minutes and already had an essay assigned.

"Hey, guys, come look," Hannah and her sunglasses announced to the class, and we all moved over to the window to see what she was so interested in. The teacher had turned on a video about the French and Indian War and then left the classroom. Yes, even in expensive private boarding schools the teachers put on videos and leave the room.

There was a rapidly growing cluster of protesters standing at the gate of the school. They were carrying signs that we couldn't make out and gesturing angrily. A pair of school security guards was walking down the steps toward them.

"What did we do?" someone asked.

"Who said we did anything?" someone replied.

"They did," Hannah said. "They're protesting something."

I pulled out my phone—which we weren't allowed to bring to class, but I was pretending I was too new to the school to remember that rule—to check the news just as a voice came over the PA. "All students and faculty please come to the auditorium."

"They're bringing them here," I said to Rachel after a quick Google search of the news.

"Who?"

"The aliens."

"You mean there are going to be aliens living here? Because they need a place for them to live? I heard they were taking over a bunch of hotels in addition to the tent city down by the ship."

"Well, they have to live somewhere. They're people."

"They're aliens," Hannah said.

"You know what I meant."

"No, I don't. They're not people. They're aliens."

I ignored her and followed the rest of the students to the auditorium.

The auditorium wasn't just the auditorium: it was the Jeffrey S. Savage Auditorium, and the stage wasn't just a stage, but the Annette Lyon Commemorative Stage. The lectern even had a name on it—somebody Eden—but it was too small for me to make out most of the words.

This was the first time I was able to get a real sense of what was left of the student body. The school was small. Like, tiny. There were maybe three hundred seats, but the seats were less than half full. Everyone was dressed neatly in their uniforms, and they must have been drilled on auditorium etiquette, because the boys sat on one side and the girls sat on the other. I kept my eye out for other girls of color. There were two black girls and four Asians. And that seemed to be it. Minnetonka School was obviously not well known for its diversity policies.

Brynne found us and sat down beside me. "Maybe the school is handing out condoms and Planned Parenthood brochures, or maybe they're going the other direction and announcing that we'll all be taking mandatory gun safety classes."

I handed my phone to Brynne. Her jaw dropped. "What the hell?"

We sat in the auditorium for more than thirty minutes. We ran out of things to talk about, except for speculating on why they would possibly be sending aliens to our school. I started to make notes of the questions I wanted to ask my dad when we had dinner on Wednesday night, assuming he hadn't forgotten that we'd made plans.

At long last, the lights dimmed, and two men in dark suits approached the stage, staying close to the wall. I glanced behind me and saw four more men dressed in similar suits with similar short haircuts—two standing by each door.

"Tell me if I'm crazy," I whispered, "but don't they look like the Secret Service?"

"It can't be the real Secret Service," Rachel said, craning her neck back to look. "They didn't check to make sure none of us are carrying weapons. If this was the real Secret Service, they'd do that, wouldn't they?"

A moment later the headmistress of the school walked out onto the stage, and all the students clapped for her. This seemed weird to me, but I wasn't fully trained in Minnetonka culture yet.

"Thank you," she said. "And thank you so much for your patience today. I know you've been left waiting for quite some time. Before we get to our main business of the day, a few announcements. First, we've had a few new students arrive in the last few days, due to the circumstances at Lakeville."

The circumstances at Lakeville? You mean the crash of an enormous UFO?

"These new students are the children of our country's best and brightest who have moved to the area to conduct research. Alice Goodwin, Heather Moore, Michele Holmes. Please stand."

I reluctantly got to my feet, looking around for the other two new girls. They looked as uncomfortable as I was. Everyone clapped, and we sat back down.

"I'm sure that you have already given a great Minnetonka

School welcome to these stellar students. Top-notch kids."

If anyone looked *really* uncomfortable, it was the headmistress.

"I'd now like to present to you Lu Ann Staheli, our fine senator from the state of Minnesota." She held out her hand, gesturing off stage. There was a pause, like no one knew what they were supposed to be doing, and then the senator appeared, her shoes clacking across the hardwood stage.

She stood at the podium, perfectly calm and collected, as if she did this every day. She probably did, I guess. The applause for her was more of what you'd call a "smattering."

"The Minnetonka School for the Gifted and Talented is known for two things—academics and citizenship. Your school produces some of the brightest scholars in our country, as well as many great leaders, in both the private and public spheres. It is this second topic I want to address with you.

"We have seen a great change in the past several days. You all heard the president address the country and the world about the growing relationship we will have with this alien race. Over the past few days we've had many diplomatic talks about how to integrate these men and women—and yes, I'm calling them men and women. They are people. They may come from another world, but we believe that they are deserving of the same inalienable rights that are granted to everyone."

Brynne shot a look at me.

I looked back, worry on my face.

"We believe that it would be a sign of goodwill—a sign of the best of mankind's intentions—to try to integrate a few of the Guides into our society."

The murmuring in the crowd was getting loud now, but Senator Staheli's smile never wavered. "It is my privilege to bring you two additional students to join the Minnetonka student body. Let me present to you, Suski and Coya."

The murmurs dropped to utter silence as two people stepped slowly out of the wings and onto the stage. They were the aliens I'd seen on TV—the first two out of the ship after Mai and the woman.

They seemed puzzled by the bright lights in their eyes, and only walked to the senator after much coaxing from the headmistress.

They both wore the school uniform, although neither wore shoes, which seemed totally out of place. Each had on a small headset, and they wore big round buttons on their sweaters, which I assumed were the speakers for their translators.

"The dude's hot," Brynne whispered, breaking the silence, and a few of the girls around us giggled. "Seriously, I think he could bench-press me."

I groaned. "Please don't say—"

"If you know what I mean," Brynne said.

"That."

"Succubus," she reminded me.

The senator stepped back to the microphone. "We will have security on-site. FBI agents inside the building and the National Guard outside. We trust that you will treat these students as you would any other student—any other foreign dignitary," she corrected.

"Freaks!"

The voice came from the male side of the room—one of those insults half-disguised as a sneeze. The senator looked into the crowd, shielding her eyes from the stage lights.

Murmurs ran through the auditorium, but if anyone knew who had said it, no one was letting on. The senator took her place at the microphone again, her voice stern and challenging. "Minnetonka was chosen because its student body can be trusted to be respectful. I know many of you are well connected and may think you're beyond reproach. But I'll have you know that none of you is as well connected as these Guides are now. They're here under the diplomatic wishes of the president. Please keep that in mind."

I tried to read the faces of the two Guide students, but they seemed like they weren't entirely sure what was going on—like they hadn't caught the insult or known what to make of it. "These are not simply two of the Guide children," the senator went on. "These are the son and daughter of Mai. We don't have a full grasp on Guide societal structure, but for now you should consider them royalty."

A girl behind me whispered a few words under her breath. "The hell we will."

"What about all the people who died?" Rachel asked me, her voice not angry, but uncertain. "What about them? Are we just supposed to forget?"

The room was getting loud, and the senator spoke again. "You will have a hundred questions, but I urge you to save them for your school leadership and not to let speculation run rampant. For now, we thank you in advance for your help in this matter. And know that we will be watching. Thank you."

The senator shook the hands of the two Guides and then left the stage, only to be replaced by the headmistress of the school.

We will be watching. Was that a threat? An admonition? It didn't sound warm and cuddly.

The headmistress started addressing the room again, but none of us were paying attention to anything she said. We had too many questions, and I don't think any of us expected the questions to be answered—at least not to our satisfaction. We still didn't even know what the Guides were. We didn't know what had happened on that ship. We didn't know what plans the president had for "integrating" the Guides into our society, or what plans the Guides had for us. Maybe that was the biggest question—we knew they wanted to teach us:

were we supposed to learn from these two? From Suski and Coya?

And why weren't they wearing shoes? They were wearing everything else. Why not shoes? Of everything going on, that pissed me off the most. I don't know why.

I was shaken from my thinking when both Rachel and Brynne looked at me, one from each side. I knew I'd missed something.

"What?" I whispered.

"Weren't you listening?" Rachel asked. "They're putting the girl in our suite—in Nikki's bed."

"You're kidding."

"There are other empty rooms," Brynne said. "Maybe they think that because your dad's in NASA, you'll be a good fit?"

"It's probably because you're both supersmart," I said. "They want to make a good impression."

"We have a new succubus," Rachel murmured, turning back to look at the girl.

She wasn't as pale as the boy, and her hair wasn't that odd shade of bleached yellow. If she'd been wearing shoes and didn't have the translator, I might have mistaken her for a human. Very probably.

I wouldn't have mistaken Suski.

Let's get one thing out of the way right up front. Yes, he looked albino, but he was a good-looking boy. Man. He was a man. I don't know how old he was, but once you get muscles like that, you're a man. His neck looked like it could do its own weight lifting.

Coya looked tough herself—broad-shouldered and built like a gymnast—but Suski was built like a god. Maybe not a Zeus or an Apollo, but certainly a demigod: a Hercules or Achilles.

Eventually, the headmistress stopped yammering on and everyone was dismissed—everyone except the people who were going to be rooming with the aliens. Brynne, Rachel, and I worked our way up to the front, and three boys I only sort of knew—Malcolm, Joshua, and Eric—came from the other side of the room. Rachel pushed me to the front, and I pushed Brynne ahead of me. She crossed the stage to where the headmistress stood with the two Guides and reached out to take Suski's hand.

"My name is Brynne," she said. "You are?"

There was a pause—I assumed the translator was working.

"Hu Suski lessina," he said. His voice was really deep. A computer voice said, with some mild inflection: "I am Suski."

Suski looked at me, then reached toward my blue hair.

"K'uirska."

"Blue," the translator said.

"Kurska," I repeated poorly, and held out my hair for him to feel.

He smiled a little at my attempt at his language as he felt

my hair between his snow-white fingers. I could see that his hands were rough and I wondered what kind of job he had on the spaceship to toughen him up so much.

I reached out my hand and he took it in his, letting my hair drop back into place. Then I pointed him to Rachel, who shook his hand eagerly.

"Rachel," she said, patting herself on the chest. She was a pale redhead and Brynne was a pale blonde; I could see that both of them fit in more with the people we'd seen emerging from the ship. But I was the dark-skinned girl with blue hair, and Coya reached out to touch it the way her brother had.

"Alice," I said to her as we moved down the line and shook her hand. Her grip was just as strong as Suski's.

"Coya," she said to me, patting her own chest, just as I had done. The translator said, "Beautiful."

"Perfect name," Brynne said.

After a moment of processing, Coya spoke, and her translator—using a female voice—said the words, "It is too much flattery. My brother's name means he is a great warrior."

"Not too much flattery. Good to know," said Brynne.

"We're going to be roommates," Rachel said to Coya. "That means we'll share a room, just the four of us."

She nodded and reached out to touch my hair again. "I would like blue in my hair."

I turned to the headmistress, who was listening to all of this. "That would be nice, don't you think?"

When we got back to our room we saw that some very helpful school administrator had taken down most of the Halloween decorations that could be construed as offensive. And admittedly, it made me look at everything in a new light. Was there a reason that we put up pictures of severed heads and rotting zombies and bloody skeletons? What was it about Halloween, and human nature, that made us revel in all things horrifying?

Our succubi banner remained in place, as did the sexy devil, because gory corpses are one thing, but scantily clad girls with tails are something else entirely. If the Guides were going to get used to modern America, they were going to need to get used to scantily clad women. Or maybe that was what they were on their interstellar trek to teach us—that we all needed to be more modest. Either way, if Coya was bothered by the succubus on the door she didn't say anything, and she didn't ask anyone to translate the word—maybe she didn't even recognize the letters as letters.

The resident assistant was with us as we showed Coya her bed, her desk—which had a brand-new laptop with her name on it—and her closet, which was filled with a week's worth of uniforms.

"We're going to have to take you shopping," Rachel told Coya as the resident assistant finally left us in peace. "We'll get you some new clothes."

"I have clothes," Coya said through the translator.

"New clothes," I said. "More clothes. Did you guys always wear the same clothes, all the time? On the spaceship?"

"Yes," Coya said, trying to respond to my question quickly to cover up the lag in translation. "Always the same clothes. I am not accustomed to these. May I ask a question?"

We all responded at once with a yes, and she smiled uncomfortably.

"How do you sit down?" she asked. "With this?" She held out the hem of her skirt.

"Oh!" Brynne said, and sat down. We all did, and Coya smiled.

"I'm not accustomed to my legs not being covered." She gingerly sat down, keeping her legs close together and holding the skirt tight against her.

"Girl," Brynne said, "you came to the right place."

We quickly assessed her sizes and dug through our drawers. Coya wasn't self-conscious about changing in front of us and quickly got out of her skirt and into a pair of designer jeans. We also switched out her top for a button-up shirt and a warm white cardigan.

"So we might as well talk about the elephant in the room,"

I said. "Why did you and the ali— your people—land here?"

Coya thought for a long time, and I exchanged glances with Rachel and Brynne.

"Why did you crash?" Rachel said, her words slowed down significantly.

Coya looked up. "I can tell you why we crashed. I just don't understand 'elephant' and how to talk about it."

We laughed, a little uncomfortably, and I said, "It's an animal. An 'elephant in the room' means that there's a big question on everyone's mind. Something everyone is thinking about."

"Animals are new to me," Coya said, still fiddling with the last buttons on her cardigan.

Brynne leaned forward. "You don't have animals on your planet?"

"I don't have a planet," Coya said. "I lived my whole life on that ship. My home."

"Seriously?"

"None of us ever lived anywhere else. Even my father, Mai."

Rachel spoke. "So, back to the elephant. Why did you come here? Why did you crash?"

"We came as Guides," Coya said, repeating the party line. "We crashed because of a malfunction with the ship. I don't know what it was. I didn't work in that part." Her lip began to quiver, but it seemed to be more out of fear than of sadness. "We didn't mean to hurt anyone. It was an accident. I promise. We didn't mean to."

Rachel stood up and wrapped Coya in a hug. "It's okay," Rachel said. "It's okay."

EIGHT

Classes the next day were uncomfortable for everyone, the teachers especially. They didn't know how to deal with aliens in the classroom, and they kept interrupting their lectures to make sure that words weren't going over their heads. AP U.S. History was the worst, because the teacher felt like he had to go back and give the backstory on everything, so while we should have been talking about the Civil War, the professor first thought that we should talk about what the South was seceding from, which meant that he had to talk about the formation of the country, which meant he had to talk about everything all the way back to the pilgrims. We were an hour into class before we got back to the Civil War, with only twenty minutes to cover such weighty topics as slavery and states' rights and economic disparity.

"Do you know economics?" the professor asked.

No.

"Do you know money?"

No.

"Let's take this lecture back a little bit further."

It mirrored a conversation we'd had earlier that morning when Coya pointed to the picture on our door and asked what a succubus is.

"Do you know the word *seduce*?" Brynne asked.

No.

"Do you know the word *flirt*?"

No.

"Do you know *romance*?"

No.

"Do you know *sex*?"

Oh yeah. That one. She knew that. Everyone knows that.

"We're not really evil monsters that have sex with boys and then kill them," Brynne had explained matter-of-factly. "But that's what we call ourselves. As a joke."

The Bruner Scholar for Uncomfortable and Awkward Silences just accepted her award.

Anyway, AP U.S. History eventually ended, and I knew that the professor was going to recommend some kind of crash course in world events for his two Guide students. He couldn't assign them extra reading, given that they couldn't read, so he told them he'd have some videos ready for them next class, and they could watch them in the library to help them catch up.

"So, tell me about Suski," Brynne said, sitting backward on her chair, her chin resting on her folded arms.

"What do you want to know?" Coya asked.

"Well," Brynne said, putting her hands up innocently, "I know he's your brother, but you've got to know he's cute."

Coya took a deep breath and furrowed her brow.

"It's true," I said. "Rachel?"

"Not my type," she said. "But I can see the draw."

"I don't understand," Coya said, getting flustered. "Why does it matter?"

"We don't have to talk about it right now," I said, and picked up a magazine. "We could take a *Cosmo* quiz."

Rachel threw a pillow at me and then turned to Coya. "Why don't you wear shoes?"

Coya looked puzzled, as though the translation didn't go through.

"Shoes," I said, and patted my black leather boots with a two-inch heel, because I'm a naughty rebel. "Why don't you wear anything on your feet?"

"Oh," Coya said, and looked uncomfortable again. It was a face she had mastered.

We all waited.

"Shoes?" I asked again.

"We don't wear those," she said. "We don't feel it is appropriate."

Appropriate? Really?

"Now wait a minute," Rachel said. "Is this a Guide thing? Like, is this one of the things that you're supposed to teach us?"

There was that awkwardness again.

"I'm not your Guide," Coya said. "That is Mai. He is our leader."

"He is your father, right?" I asked.

She slowly nodded her head. "He is my father. Suski is my brother. I have many other brothers and sisters."

"What about your mother?" Brynne asked.

"I do not know 'mother.' That is not a thing that we have," Coya said.

"What?" Rachel said. "Everyone has a mother. We all have mothers."

I spoke up. "My mother is dead. Is that what you mean? Your mother is dead?"

"I don't know. I don't have one of those."

Rachel jumped in. "Is this some kind of commune thing? The kids are raised by all the women, and mothers don't take care of their own babies?"

"I don't know 'commune,'" Coya said, looking confused.

"We did see children coming out of the ship," Rachel

said, her voice almost desperate. "I don't remember if they were with mothers."

"Who raised you?" I asked. "Who took care of you when you were little?"

"I'm not sure I understand," Coya said, and her discomfort turned to defensiveness. "What do you mean 'take care of'?"

"Who taught you?" Brynne asked. She stood up and began changing out of her uniform. "Who made sure the kids had food to eat?"

"We all did," Coya said. "We all taught children."

Brynne pulled on a Kansas State sweatshirt. "But when a woman had a baby, wasn't she in charge of that baby? Didn't she teach the baby?"

Coya shook her head. "I don't want to talk about this."

"You have a brother—Suski. Does he have the same mother as you?"

"I want to talk to Suski," she said. "Where is he?"

"We'll take you to him," Brynne said, standing up slowly. "But answer the question. When a woman had a baby, what happened to the baby?"

"Everyone taught the baby," Coya said, standing up and folding her arms. "Everyone loved the baby. This is good."

"Fine," Rachel said. "We'll take you to see Suski." She stood up and rummaged in her closet before pulling out a pair of very simple leather sandals. "But you have to wear these."

"And," Brynne said, holding out a long Q-Tip, "this is a tradition. Open your mouth."

"What is this?" Coya said.

"Aaaaah," Brynne said, and soon Coya was mimicking the expression. Quickly Brynne swabbed the inside of the alien's cheek and dropped the Q-tip into a test tube.

We sat in the common room, me with a bowl of ice cream, Brynne with a bowl of blueberries, and Rachel with an enormous wedge of chocolate cream pie. Of the three of us, she seemed the most outraged by the mother issue, although none of us were happy about it.

Suski and Coya were in the cafeteria at a table by the window, a plate of food in front of each of them that they weren't touching. Coya had the sandals on her feet. I hadn't seen if Suski had reacted to them, but in all the time I sat staring at the two Guides, he never looked.

His roommates hadn't taken the time to dress him like we'd done with Coya, so he sat there looking sullen in his blazer and khakis and bare feet. He was talking quietly to his sister, both of their translator earpieces removed and lying on the table.

"Who would think," Brynne began, "that a vastly advanced race of supposedly superior beings would be so conservative? They don't think it's appropriate to wear shoes? Is that why they all wore the same clothes, too? Is it some kind of Amish antifashion thing?"

"Maybe it's the opposite," Rachel said. "Maybe it's not conservative, but liberal. Maybe the lack of differentiation is because they're all equal and no one should dress any better than anyone else."

"That doesn't explain the shoe thing."

"No."

Suski's eyes met mine, and I immediately looked away, embarrassed that I was staring at him. He turned back to Coya and said something. She nodded. He didn't look happy. Maybe he was pissed that we'd given his sister new clothes. Brynne stood and stretched. "Let me know if something interesting happens. I'm going back to study. I want to get that cheek swab going soon."

"I should really be studying," Rachel said. "The Princeton Math Competition is coming up, and I'm trying to get on the team." She took another bite of pie.

"You all work too hard."

"It helps me relax, though."

"Then all of this work has driven you crazy."

"It's something we have in common with them," she said, gesturing to Suski and Coya with her fork. "Math. It's the one language that everyone has in common, because math is math. Pi is always pi. One plus one always equals two."

"Maybe if they ever get past telling us not to wear shoes, they'll pass along some of that knowledge."

"I hope so," she said, and took another bite.

"Not that you need help," I said. "You're freaking brilliant."

"That's all relative," Rachel said absently. "You can be brilliant in the first grade because you know all your multiplication tables. But that doesn't compare to being brilliant in junior high or being brilliant in college. These guys probably just raised the bar. They'll have new math. New, amazing stuff that will make our Nobel Prize winners look like those first graders. They must. You can't have a ship that advanced and not have figured out some amazing things."

"That doesn't make you any less brilliant," I said. "You'll just have more material to learn from. I bet Coya doesn't know all the math that made the ship fly, or how to put it together. It's not something that every alien would just know. It's still a specialized skill. It's probably the engineers who are working with my dad—they're the really smart ones."

"Either way, my point is that we have at least one thing in common—math." She stood up. "I'm going back to the room. Text me if anything interesting happens. If Suski caresses your hair again or something."

She grinned and headed toward the dorm. My eyes met Suski's again, but I held the stare this time, and he was the one to look away.

"You're shedding friends," a voice said behind me, and I looked up to see Kurt. He hopped over the couch and plopped down next to me. "People are beginning to talk."

"You know," I said, "I've been in this school for less than a week. People should still be coming up to introduce themselves to me, not leaving me to wander the room getting to know people."

"That's not what they teach in the networking seminar," he said.

"There's seriously a networking seminar? Of course there is. I'd forgotten where I was."

"You have to work the room, like a cocktail party."

"I don't go to a lot of cocktail parties."

"Then work it like a high school dance," he said. "Move around the room. Talk to people. Exchange business cards. Swap golf stories."

"So, what do you think," I said, gesturing to the Guides with my now-empty ice cream bowl. "Coya in Brynne's clothes. You think she could pass for a human?"

"Absolutely," he said. "Nicely done, by the way. Dressing her, I mean."

"You think we could do the same thing with Suski? Or is he just too, well, alien?"

"He looks albino. I bet any humans who are real albinos right now are getting a lot of crap." He cocked his head to one side and looked at her. "But Coya—platinum blond hair. Fair skin. Brynne's got more of a tan, but not much. I personally think Brynne's hotter—"

"Shut up."

"You asked."

"Yeah, whatever." I stood up.

"Where are you going? What if I say that you're prettier than Brynne?"

"I'd say you're lying through your teeth."

"I'm not."

"Whatever."

"Where are you going?"

"I'm going to dye a blue streak in Coya's hair."

I sat down at the table with Suski and Coya. They put their earpieces back in and stared at me.

"Hello, Alice," Coya said. I liked her language: "*Guw'aadzi*, Alice."

"Gooadsee," I said back to her, and they both smiled warily.

I looked at Suski and took Coya's hand. "I need to borrow your sister."

He narrowed his eyes. "I'm not sure I understand."

"I need Coya to come with me. We're going to go hang out with the girls. Is that okay, Coya?"

She pulled her hand away suspiciously. "What do you mean by 'hang out'?"

I touched my blue hair. "You said you wanted blue in your hair?"

Her face slowly changed from suspicion to worry to tentative pleasure. She looked at Suski, like she needed his approval. He said something in their language, clearly displeased, and the translator automatically interpreted it for me.

"You said they were angry with you."

"They were angry with life on the ship. They don't understand."

Suski realized I was listening and turned off both his and Coya's translators. He talked sternly for a good two minutes.

"Does your translator know the word *patriarchal* yet?" I asked, knowing they couldn't understand me.

They looked at each other and then back at me, and then Suski returned to his speech.

"Well, good. You seem to have a very patriarchal society." I smiled as I said it so that maybe they'd think it was a compliment, and after a moment, Suski forced a smile back.

I took Coya's hand and stood up. She followed me and turned her translator back on.

We hurried back to the girls' dorm, and I burst into our room, already kicking off my shoes and unbuttoning my shirt.

"What's going on?" Rachel asked, sitting at her desk. She really was studying math, two pencils holding her hair up. I couldn't understand her.

"Help me," I said. "We're giving Coya a blue streak."

I heard Brynne's voice from the other bedroom. "What?" A moment later she appeared. "I am so getting involved. You have dye?"

I pulled on a T-shirt that I didn't mind ruining, and then fumbled through my luggage until I found the slightly beat-up box of Blistering Blue. "I brought it along to clean up my roots, but it sounds like that won't be happening."

"Sweet," Brynne said, opening the box to see how much was there. "Coya's hair's long, but this should work fine. Rachel, can you run down to the kitchen and ask for some tinfoil?"

We didn't take long—Brynne was a seasoned professional, and Coya was a good canvas to work on. After Brynne dyed the streak into Coya's long hair and wrapped it in tinfoil, I set to work on Coya's makeup. She freaked out at the eyeliner pencil, but everyone does that at first and I couldn't blame her. After twenty minutes we moved her in front of the mirror, and she smiled uncertainly. To finish off the look, we gave her a warm winter sweater and a pair of Brynne's designer jeans. We couldn't talk her into better shoes, not even when we told her how cold it was outside, but overall the look still worked. I felt a little bit like a mother watching her little girl getting her first haircut. Everything was new and scary to Coya—especially when Brynne opened the foil and rinsed and rinsed, and rinsed some more, and then began to towel it dry with a thick old red tattered thing.

"I thought you weren't supposed to dye blond hair?" Rachel said. "I think I read that in one of your magazines."

"There's nothing wrong with it," Brynne answered, "it's just that you can't dye it out. You can't bleach it. You get weird blue and green."

"I love my hair," Coya said, beaming. "I love blue."

"So what do we do now?" Rachel asked.

"I think we go back to the cafeteria and get something to eat. Show her off." I looked at Coya. "Suski is going to be there."

Coya's hand gripped the edge of her desk, staring through the small window at the end of the room. "What is that?"

"Nothing," I said. "Just the back of the school. You can see the track—for running."

"What is falling?"

"Oh," Rachel answered excitedly. "That's snow. It's frozen water."

"I love it," Coya said, with wonder in her voice.

To be honest, I was almost in as much awe as she was. The only place I ever saw snow was at my *Shimasani*'s home in New Mexico, but that snow always melted quickly. My grandma and grandpa Goodwin got a lot of snow, but we usually visited them in the summer.

"We can go the back way to the cafeteria," Rachel said.

"What back way?" Brynne asked.

"C'mon," Rachel said with a smile as she led the way into

the hall. "There's a door out here that I use to avoid, well, people."

She led us twenty feet out of our room to a steel door marked "Electrical Room." I would have assumed it was locked, but Rachel turned the knob and we entered a small, dark room. I lost her in the darkness for an instant and then saw her outline and felt a rush of cold air.

"This goes outside?"

"Yep," she said, pushing the door open against the slushy snow on the patio. "This goes all the way around past the gym and the cafeteria and to the parking lot."

"I do not like this place's feeling on my skin," Coya said.

It took us a minute to get it, but Brynne was the first to figure it out. "The cold, you mean? I guess you guys never had changing weather."

A shock of ice hit my neck and zapped down my spine. I spun to see Brynne and Rachel both laughing.

"Which one of you did it?" I said, trying to get the clump of snow out of my shirt. "Rachel, I know it was you. You're dead."

"It wasn't me," she said, holding up her hands in an *I'm as innocent as Mother Teresa* look. Brynne gave me the same look.

"You're both dead, then," I said.

"What do you mean?" Coya asked. "They are not dead."

I laughed, still unable to get the snow out from under my coat. It was soaking into my waistband. "It's just a saying," I told her. "It means they're in trouble."

"Oh," she said, suddenly serious. "I understand dead. They are not dead."

"No," I said. "And they're not even in trouble. It's a joke."

"It seems a strange thing to joke about," she said, and then drew her fingers through her hair again. "I love this blue."

We walked around the back of the school in mostly silence. Coya asked a few questions about the snow—how much would fall, how soon it would melt—which Rachel answered. I kept thinking about what Coya had said about death. She understood death.

When we got to the common room door, it was locked. Rachel looked heartbroken, like the one thing she was good at had gone wrong. I pulled out my phone and called Kurt.

"Hey, want to rescue four freezing girls?"

He laughed. "Where are you?"

"At the common room's outside door."

"I swear, Goodwin, you'll owe me for this one."

"Because it's really hard to open a door."

"Is there a good reason for you to be out there?"

"Just open the door."

"I can see you from here," he said, and hung up.

As he walked toward us, a few glances came in our direction, and when he opened the door, at least a dozen people were looking at us.

"I don't think we've achieved much avoiding the crowd, Rachel," I said.

"Are you kidding?" Brynne said. "I just learned how to get out of the building without even sneaking past the RA. That's gold."

Coya stopped, shivering. "Does this snow come often?"

"Half the year," Rachel said. "So, yeah. A lot."

"I think . . . ," Coya said. "I think I will wear shoes."

NINE

The FBI must have placed alarms on all the doors, because one of the agents appeared almost immediately in the common room, talking into his radio. Soon we were sitting in the headmistress's office getting a lecture on safety and responsibility.

"I entrusted you girls with the care of this young woman," she said, in that voice that adults use when they want to show how disappointed they are with your behavior. "This isn't a game. Life and death are on the line. You've seen the protestors."

"She looks human. And we were outside for maybe five minutes, not to mention we were nowhere near the front gates," I said.

"It was still irresponsible," she said, which I think was her way of saying I'd won but she didn't care. "Your parents will be notified. Coya will be assigned to a different room—to girls who are more trustworthy."

I opened my mouth to say something, but Coya spoke.

"I want to stay with Alice and Rachel and Brynne."

The headmistress smiled at her—she didn't want to make the guest unhappy, but she wanted to punish us all just the same. "I'm sure we can find another situation that is a better fit."

"This is a good fit," Coya said with newfound fierceness. "I like these three girls. They protect me."

The headmistress sighed and leaned back in her chair. Her eyes met mine, and then she glanced at Rachel and Brynne. "You realize that this kind of misbehavior could hurt your chances of becoming Bruner Scholars. Part of the scholarship is based on leadership and citizenship."

"Yes, ma'am," they chorused, more cowed than me. I didn't have as much to lose.

"I'll be watching you more closely," the headmistress finally said. "And, Coya, you have my apologies. This should never have happened."

"This was a good thing," Coya said. "I liked it."

She gave us all one last disapproving look. "You're dismissed."

We stood up from the plush leather chairs opposite her desk. Coya's face broke into a big smile. "Headmistress, do you like my hair? It's blue, like Alice's."

She nearly choked on her sigh. "Yes. Very nice."

We managed to get outside and wait for her office door to shut before we started laughing.

Coya wanted to find Suski to show him her hair, so we headed back to the cafeteria. Suski was still sitting at the same table. It didn't look like he'd moved an inch. The tray of lunch he hadn't eaten had been replaced with a tray of dinner he wasn't eating. When he saw Coya, he stood up, obviously upset.

They spoke together in their own language, not waiting for their translators, and it was hard to follow the conversation as the machines struggled to keep up.

"Where have you been?"

"—getting blue in my—"

"—just do this without—"

"—safe and with my—"

"—not safe. You don't know what this place is like. You don't know who these people are. You don't—"

"—not Father. I was—"

"—dangerous. I demand that you obey."

She stared back at him, and then made a gesture with both fists knocking together. She spun and looked back at me. "Let's go to the room."

I nodded and gave Suski a hard look, which he returned. Rachel took Coya by the hand, which seemed to surprise her at first, but then she smiled weakly.

I turned to Kurt. "I'll catch up with you later, okay?"

"Sure. I'm not going anywhere."

I headed after Rachel, Brynne, and Coya, who were already out of the cafeteria and down the hallway. We entered the dorm and passed the RA's room, but she didn't glance up.

"Is he always like that?" I asked Coya. "So serious?"

"Yes," she said. "Suski is always serious."

"Why?" Rachel asked.

"He's had a hard life," Coya said. "He doesn't trust you aliens—humans."

I laughed. "I've never thought about that. We're aliens to you."

We opened the door to our room, and Brynne flopped down on a couch, picking up a magazine. Of course, it wasn't *Cosmo* or something fun like that. It was *The Journal of Human Genetics*.

"You are such a nerd," I said.

"Such a frustrated nerd," she said, looking again at Coya's hair. "I love it. It should be a succubus thing. We should all do it. What do you think, Rach?"

"Alas," Rachel said, "I think we'd better toe the line after the *You're not going to win the Bruner if you act like this* talk from the headmistress."

"Ugh."

I turned to Brynne. "You could probably dye your whole

head a rainbow and still get the Bruner. There's no one in biology that comes close to you."

"You only say that because you haven't been here very long," Rachel said. "What the headmistress said was true—a lot of the scholarship is about being a good citizen, which means following the rules. They want geniuses, but they want geniuses who will give the school a good name."

Coya spoke. "I don't understand. The blue is a bad thing?"

"Not for you," I said. "And not for me. Do you know the term *double standard*?"

"No."

Brynne answered. "It means that Rachel and I are trying to win an award, and we won't win it if we have blue in our hair."

"I don't understand 'award,'" Coya said.

We spent the rest of the evening explaining words to Coya, trying to teach her our culture. It was amazing the things that she didn't have any concept of: awards, winning, competition, prizes. For her, life was about work, and everyone worked and everyone got the same reward for their work, and the only surprises were unpleasant—accidents, death. Crashing into Iowa.

She didn't have much of a story to explain how they crashed. She had never even been to the control room of the ship—the bridge, or the cockpit, or whatever they called it. All our attempts at explaining that word didn't register with her. She had spent her life in the outer rings of the ship, working. We asked her what kind of working, and other than a vague description of cleaning, she didn't really have an answer.

Coya was not a good storyteller.

"Everyone just lived together?" Rachel asked. "No separate rooms, like our room here?"

"No," she said. "My people live together. All together. No, I am wrong. There are many rooms like this room—many rooms for people to sleep in. But never a room with just two people. Never."

"What about Mai?" Brynne asked, a little suspicion in her voice. We were all getting the impression that Mai lived in some kind of luxury with a harem of women. But Coya denied it.

"Mai lived in my room," she said. "With all my brothers and sisters."

"What does this mean?" I asked, typing a few keystrokes into Google and turning my laptop screen for her to see. It was the door they'd all come out through—I pointed to the alien language written above the opening.

"I don't understand."

"Is this writing?"

"I don't know," she said, and pointed to the image. "Not that. Not those pictures."

"What are the pictures, then?"

Coya got that uncomfortable look again. She could be the Bruner Scholar for Discomfort. "I don't know. They are just pictures. They are pretty."

I looked back at the laptop. The symbols were blocky, with sharp angles and small twists. They didn't look pretty to me at all. And they didn't look like art.

"They have to be letters," I said, and tapped on the screen. "Look, this one is the same as this other one. They are some kind of writing."

"Or a repeating design," Brynne said, with a sigh that made it sound like she didn't believe that herself. She turned back to Coya. "Do you know anyone who can read?"

"I don't understand 'reading,'" Coya said.

"Reading," Brynne said, and held up her magazine and made a box with her fingers around the letter *T*. "This is a *T*. It sounds like this: *t-t-t-t*. Then this is an *H*. It sounds like *h-h-h-h*. So together—wait, why did I choose *the*?"

Coya shook her head. "I don't understand."

"What about math?" Rachel said, grabbing four pens from her desk. She laid them on the bed. "One, two, three, four."

Coya took the four remaining pens and continued, and I listened to her language: *"Taam'a, sh'isa, maityana, kukyum'ishi."* The translator followed with "five, six, seven, eight."

There was something familiar about the words. I only knew English and a little bit of Navajo, and this definitely wasn't either, but it sounded like something I'd heard before.

Rachel laid out two pens and then two more. "Two pens and two pens is . . ."

Coya paused for a moment. *"Dyaana."* And her translator said, "Four."

Rachel took a deep, calming breath, as though everything was going to be okay now because Coya could do arithmetic. But I was hatching a plan. I was going to find Suski and show him the letters from the picture. See if he could read them. I wanted to see just what kind of patriarchy we were dealing with where barefoot girls didn't have mothers and weren't even able to read. And then, depending on how it went, maybe I'd show him some of the self-defense moves Dad insisted I master before I could date. Mostly jujitsu.

Then again, it wasn't just barefoot girls. It was barefoot everybody. But still.

Sometimes I think I hatch too many plans.

So, instead of going on a mission, I pulled out my copy of *Cosmo* and we took the first quiz: "What Kind of Female Are You?" Despite the stilted name—and having to explain to Coya what the point of a *Cosmo* quiz is—we began. *How do you feel about your job?* None of us had jobs, so we used school as a stand-in. Rachel chose *Love it, seriously.* Brynne did, too, and I couldn't believe I was rooming with such losers. I picked *It's fine, but I don't work more than I have to.* And Coya finally picked *It's a job, it's necessary.*

I won't bore you with the rest of the details, but Brynne

got *Experience First* and Rachel got *Love First* and I got *Figuring It Out.* That stung a little bit, but I guess it's true. Coya got *Career First,* which we all laughed at since she didn't even know what *career* meant.

Then, lest it turn into too much of a slumber party, I told them I needed to sleep. The day had been a whirlwind, and I was ready for peace and quiet. I think I was asleep before I even pulled the covers over me.

The next evening I found Suski at his usual table, picking a little at his steamed broccoli. The way he always sat there made me wonder if he was used to sitting in one place, like a king holding court or something like that.

"A lot of people don't like broccoli," I said, inviting myself to sit.

"It looks the most like the food we ate at our home. What did you call it? Broccaa?"

"Broccoli," I said, and I pointed to an empty spot on his plate, where the remnants of some dark sauce remained. "What was that?"

"Very good, just like a food we have. Fungus."

I was repulsed for a moment and then laughed. "Mushrooms! You like mushrooms. I bet they would grow well in a giant dark ship."

"We never put this liquid on them."

"You can go back and get more."

"I don't want to take more than my share."

"We never run out of mushrooms," I said. "Hang on."

I set all my stuff on the table—my laptop and my backpack—and I grabbed a plate and jogged to the long buffet. There were people getting food, but not enough that it looked like I was cutting in line. The dish I was looking for was marked with a card: "Wild Mushrooms in Red Wine Sauce." It was supposed to be a sauce for the steak nearby, but if Suski just wanted to eat gravy, at least he was eating something. I filled up the dish with it and carried it back to him.

"For you," I said.

For the first time he looked at me with a smile that felt real, but it quickly faded.

"Coya says you have been rude to her."

"About what?"

"About the way we live on the ship. About not knowing who gave us birth."

"You know who your fathers are."

He stabbed a mushroom with his fork and ate it, chewing with his mouth slightly open. "Our people are different than your people."

"Okay, okay," I said, stopping that line of questioning—for now, at least. "Can I show you a picture?"

"Fine," he said.

I opened my laptop and quickly found the photos with the lettering. I turned the computer toward him.

"Do you know what this means?"

He looked for a long time. "I don't understand your question."

"Do you know how to read?"

He turned and reached into his bag. I started to get excited, wondering what amazing thing could possibly be in there. Maybe a reading translator, like his speech translator?

He pulled out a thin graphic novel, with a spaceship on the cover. *Schlock Mercenary* by Howard Tayler. "The English teacher is trying to teach me how to read English. She thinks this spaceship funny book will be easier for me, but it is not."

I tapped the screen at the writing above the door the guides had cut their way through. "So you don't think these designs here mean anything."

"Are they for reading?"

I put my forehead in my hands. "Yes." Why did he—the son of Mai, the leader—not recognize the language on the ship?

"Coya said you guys never left the ship, right?"

He nodded, chewing on another mushroom.

"Then maybe that writing is not for you, but for someone else?"

"Possibly."

"Why don't you have mothers?"

"What?"

"You have a father. What about a mother?"

His lips straightened into a tight line, and he pushed the mushrooms away. "Is this what you attacked Coya about?"

"We didn't attack Coya. We just talked to her about it."

"She felt betrayed."

I felt my stomach drop. "That wasn't our intention. Not at all."

"Coya is a good girl," he said. "We did not come to this school to be treated poorly. We are the children of Mai."

"Well—" But he interrupted me.

"I do not know what is on the outside of the ship. I have never looked at the outside of the ship until we came to this planet. I didn't know we were even on a ship. I didn't know what a ship was. I thought I was in my home."

"What?" Just then my phone buzzed, and I snatched it up. "Hi, Dad."

"The FBI has me surrounded."

"I'll be right out." I slid my laptop back into my backpack, said good-bye to Suski, and headed to the school's front entrance. Dad was standing there, looking at a display case of inventions created by former Minnetonka students. He was flanked by two frowning FBI agents.

"Aly," Dad said, and gave me a hug. He had shaved and was even wearing a clean shirt. I was impressed.

"You didn't have to go all out," I said. "I kind of expected you to be grizzled and covered with coffee stains."

"I'm taking my daughter to dinner," he said. "I can at least shave and put on deodorant. I even showered. I know you're doubting me."

One of the FBI agents spoke up. "She's not allowed to leave the property."

"Excuse me?" I said, just as Dad said, "What? Why not?"

"Orders from above," the FBI agent said. "Just yesterday she snuck out of the building with one of the aliens."

"Aly," Dad said. I couldn't tell if it was his real disappointed voice or his fake one.

"We were outside for maybe three minutes," I said.

"All I know," the agent said, "is that we have new orders. If students leave they cannot come back in."

"Want to join me in the cafeteria?" I asked.

Dad looked down at me. "It would be an honor."

"They're serving deep-fried walleye. It's a fish," I said. "I looked it up. It's called 'walleye' because its eyes point out to the sides, like it's looking at the walls. The opposite of cross-eyed. And they're serving steak with a mushroom sauce that one of the Guides really likes."

"Really? Which one?"

"The boy."

"I bet he does. They live off the stuff. We've found huge mushroom cultivation chambers. They grow well inside the ship."

"He also eats anything that looks like pureed vegetables. I think they must have eaten algae?"

"And here I thought you weren't learning anything."

"Oh, I've learned tons of stuff here. Tons. Did you know that in *Call of Duty: Black Ops*, if you shoot all the mannequin heads really fast, you can get to a secret level? I'm telling you, this is a quality education."

"Wow."

"You have to be in multiplayer."

"I'll remember that," he said. "This is a nice cafeteria. But, well, seafood in Minnesota?" he said, shaking his head.

"I'm craving it," I said.

"Lead on."

The cook behind the counter fried us some fresh fish and some chips to go with it. Dad wouldn't take one of the desserts, so I took two cherry pies—his favorite—and set one on his side of the table. He did, however, get a few pieces of pickled herring. Probably just to gross me out.

As he dipped his hot walleye into tartar sauce, he spoke. "So where are your Guides? I can't pick them out in this sea of pasty-white Minnesotans."

"Suski is sitting alone at his table over your left shoulder. And Coya is probably not eating dinner. She's a lot more liberal than her brother. Not liberal in the way that a scientist hippie who grew up in San Francisco is liberal. But she's liberal in the sense that we got her to wear shoes, and she hangs out and takes *Cosmo* quizzes and goes to parties."

Dad turned his head to cough into his arm and presumably

got a look at the ever stoic Suski.

"They don't wear shoes?"

"I know! Crazy, right? They're not very guiding. Listen to this: they don't wear shoes, they don't have mothers—what does that even mean?—and they don't know how to read."

"They don't know how to read?"

"That shocks you more than the mothers thing?"

"Different cultures do different things," he said. "Even Plato said we didn't need mother-child attachment. But they should be able to read. You'd think a star-faring race would emphasize education."

"I know!"

"Honestly, we've noticed the same thing with the engineers we've been working with. They know how to run the engines—which are surprisingly complicated and take a lot of manpower—but we haven't been able to get much of substance from them as to how anything works. They know their jobs, but they aren't pouring out great wisdom."

"But you're learning a lot, right?"

"Oh, sure," he said. "Tons. We're just having to do most of the figuring out on our own."

"So what about all the big questions?" I asked, glancing at him. "Faster-than-light travel? Their mission? What that ship is made of that allowed it to skid for nearly three hundred miles and not break up?"

He rubbed a hand over his face tiredly. "I wish. But we

have their engines. And somewhere, in that giant sea of Guides, there's someone who knows how they work. We just have to figure out who. My guess is this: all the real knowledge is being saved as bargaining chips by this Mai guy. The real scientists are just blending in until we reach some deals."

"Then we ought to start reaching some deals," I said.

"No kidding. Days are dragging on, and things aren't going well—not for us, not for them. It's got to be getting pretty miserable in that shantytown where they're living."

"It's not going to be getting much better anytime soon," I said. "It's not like we have an entire empty city where we can move them."

"And I don't know if you've been following the news, but all the federal money is going to victims of the crash first. They haven't approved anything for the Guides."

"I can't say that I blame them," I said.

"Congress is flailing," he said. "Mai is the only person from the Guides who is talking—it's not like they have a secretary of state and a vice president. It all just seems to be Mai."

"What about that woman who came out of the ship with Mai?"

"Right now it's the president and Mai."

"And in the meantime, the people are going crazy. We had a hundred protestors out in front of the school today."

"You were headline news yesterday. I'm not surprised."

"I'm sharing a room with one of them," I said.

"And are you being a good roommate?"

"I am being a *model* roommate. And she's a model roommate. They're totally normal people—and I use that word intentionally. They're people, just like any other kind of people. You wouldn't know the difference between her and me, except for my abundance of melanin."

He raised his eyebrows. "Oh, really?"

"We dyed her hair, to match mine."

"What?"

"She loved the streak in my hair, and she said she wanted one—and, like good friends and roommates, we dyed her hair and then snuck her around the back of the building to avoid the RA."

"If I didn't know you were a good kid, I'd be terrified."

"What makes you think I'm a good kid?"

"Because a bad kid would lie about sneaking out and getting caught."

After we finished eating, Dad jokingly asked for a beer and the cafeteria amazingly had not only one, but a selection. I'd forgotten that they served all the adults, too. I ordered coffee and alternately steamed my hands and sipped at it.

"Okay, Alice," he said, once he had half a bottle of microbrew in him. "I have a proposal."

I nodded for him to continue.

"This is between you and your closest friends—the two girls in your dorm room, the ones you keep saying are so smart."

"They're way smart—one of them at math and one at genetics."

"Okay, here's my problem: that ship is enormous." He took another long swallow of his beer. "You're a responsible kid."

"Very."

"And you get good grades. You're going to college."

I wondered how potent that microbrew was, but I agreed and kept listening.

"And your two roommates sound like they're just counting down time until graduation."

"Brynne already has offers to skip senior year and go to college. And Rachel's like a math savant."

"Then that does it," he said.

"That does what?"

"Get some cameras and come down to the crash site. We have a lot of people from NASA there, and we've recruited kids from the University of Minnesota, but we need more people on the ground to help us document it."

"What? Really?"

"Here's the deal: we've heard rumors from Washington that the United Nations is trying to take over the crash site, but we want the first crack at it. We want to map it and understand the technology and photograph everything, and it's so big that we can't do it all with the manpower we have. We estimate that so far we've explored about 15 percent of it. It doesn't help that the hull is round, so we need climbers to get at half of it."

"So you're inviting me and my friends to go inside the ship?" I confirmed, giddy to tell Rachel and Brynne.

"And work, yes."

"When can we start?"

"Tomorrow."

"That's perfect. I've been tracking it online, and Bluebell is supposed to get here in the morning. But you're going to have to clear this with the headmistress and the FBI."

Dad pulled out one of his NASA business cards. "These tend to get me what I want."

I grabbed my phone to call Rachel so that she and Brynne could come down and hear the news. The two of them were jogging around the corner in their pajamas in less than a minute. Brynne looked gorgeous as always, and Rachel had her hair in curlers—although she didn't seem to care if anyone saw her that way.

They sat down at the table, and I couldn't keep the grin off my face.

"Dad wants us to go inside the ship."

Brynne's jaw dropped, and Rachel squealed.

"Oh yeah," I said. "This is my dad."

Brynne stood up and shook his hand. "Brynne Fuller."

Rachel reached across the table. "I'm Rachel," she said, too dumbfounded to even give her last name.

"What's it like down there?" Brynne asked. "I mean, we've been watching the news, but what's it really like?"

"It's not a pretty sight," he said. "I don't know what the count is up to, but it looks like a sea of endless tents. I think every Porta-Potty in Minnesota is there."

"Meaning they . . . do their business just like people do?" I asked. I'd been the one who'd had to explain toilets to Coya, and it was much harder than I would have expected.

"They're just like humans from head to toe, as far as our researchers have gathered. Their translators are getting really good, but I'm not privy to all the interesting conversations."

"Why not? You're director of special projects!" Rachel said.

"My job is entirely based on the ship. Too bad it's getting pretty rotten in there. Remember a couple years ago when a cruise ship lost power and kind of drifted around at sea for an extra week, and none of the water pumps worked so none of the toilets worked?"

I made a face. "Gross."

"That's kind of the picture that we're getting from inside the ship. Want to know how many Guides were on it?"

"Sure."

"Fifty-five thousand."

Rachel spoke. "Really? We'd guessed one thirty."

He laughed, and then finally took a bite of his cherry pie. I knew he'd eat it. I win. "I came up with that same number on the plane. But, nope, it's less. Still, fifty-five thousand. That's a lot."

"What else is on the ship? If there're eighty thousand fewer Guides than you thought?"

"I've actually gotten to talk to a few of the Guides who worked in engineering," he said. "They have some words that don't translate, which means they're probably terms that we don't have in English—new, alieny things like dilithium crystals or beryllium spheres. Do you realize what kind of advances we'll be able to make in our space program based off the ship alone, not to mention their engineering minds? It's amazing!"

I talked with my mouth full of pie. "You sound like a kid on Christmas."

"This is better than Christmas," Rachel said, looking at me like I was crazy.

"So we'll be doing what on the ship?" Brynne asked. "Just taking pictures?"

"Yep," he said. "But I'll explain all of that tomorrow."

"Is it safe?" Rachel asked.

"I'll only send you to safe areas," Dad said in a gentle voice. "We're going to need an army of monkeys to fully explore this thing because so much of it is upside down, but right now we're just focusing on the bottom couple of floors, so there won't be much climbing. You'll get dizzy. And if you are prone to throwing up, you might throw up. We've found some rooms where people got pretty injured—a lot of dried blood—and some other rooms that were used as temporary bathrooms. But nothing dangerous."

"Sounds good to me!" Brynne exclaimed, and Rachel nodded vigorously.

Despite the girls' enthusiasm, there was something weird about the way my dad was acting. I knew him too well. He was hiding something.

He stood up and the girls thanked him and shook his hand.

I took his arm and walked him to the door.

"I think you're getting too excited about this," I told him. "Promise me one thing: you won't fall in love with some pretty Guide engineer and get married, because that would be the worst kind of wicked stepmother. An alien wicked stepmother."

"Aly."

"Promise me."

"Pinkie swear," he said, and held up his little finger. I yanked his pinkie with mine.

"Good. And no pinkie swearing with the pretty Guide engineers. I've seen their tight outfits. What's the deal with those, by the way?"

"Not sure. They're not the mummy wrappings they

looked like on TV. When you're up close they look more like strips of cloth all sewn together. Very weird."

"They seem to be designed for wardrobe malfunctions." I didn't know how to get him to spill.

"They do. The Guides don't seem to care, though. Or, at least, they don't seem to know anything different. Have you seen all the wounded?"

"Of course. It's hard to watch TV and *not* see them."

"Imagine you were in a spaceship going nine hundred feet per second and you hit the ground. The only way they survived is by skimming like a rock across water. It slowed them down. It was a crash landing, but it was a really amazing crash landing. They totally could have made a crater out of Iowa if they didn't know what they were doing."

"Dad, you're doing your *Wait, there's more* voice."

He frowned. "Deep inside the ship, in the heart, as far as we can tell, there was a mass suicide. We think it was the only one. But I want you guys to be ready."

"How many?" I asked, feeling like I'd just been punched in the chest.

"We're still counting, but it looks like it will be more than a thousand. And the strangest part? Sometimes they stabbed themselves in the heart or slit their own throat or slashed their wrists, but all of them—every single one—had a wound in their abdomen.

"Think about it—a spaceship crashes going Mach One,

and eighty percent of the injuries are puncture wounds to the abdomen, after which they killed themselves. It's just so weird. It has to be a clue."

"Why don't you ask somebody?"

"Like I said, they don't tell us much."

"That's superweird."

"It is," he said, and looked at his watch.

"Go, have your nerd fun," I said.

"You follow the rules."

"How much trouble can I get in between now and tomorrow morning?"

"I don't want to think about it."

When we got to the admin office, it was locked, but there was a night number for the secretary posted.

Dad talked to the secretary, who then gave him the headmistress's home number. He explained the situation and all of the great press the school could get for this, and before the call was over, the headmistress had offered to let us visit the crash site *and* to buy $3,000 cameras for the three of us girls. Score.

"Agents," Dad said when we got to the front door, "tomorrow evening I'm taking my daughter and her two roommates with me onto the ship. They will be gone for several hours. Oh, also, her car is being delivered, so it needs to be allowed through the gate. The headmistress will brief you on all of this in the morning, and I'll contact the FBI office just so we're all on the same page."

The agents didn't seem used to taking orders from civilians, but they nodded. "If you clear it with them," one of them said, "then we'll be okay."

Dad hugged me, and it was the first time I noticed he was still holding the cup of pickled herring.

"You only eat two bites of pie, but you take the herring?"

"The pie was on a ceramic plate. This is a disposable cup."

"Gross, Dad. Gross."

"Love you, Aly."

"You, too."

When I made it back to the cafeteria, Brynne sat on the couch giving a neck rub to Malcolm, who was sitting at her feet and blasting the hell out of pixelated aliens on the TV. Rachel was curled up on an oversized chair, staring at the sudoku puzzle in the newspaper like she was doing it in her head. Maybe she was. Was that possible?

I crossed the room and sat down at Suski's table. He was in no mood to talk to me, and I wasn't sure I wanted to talk to him. A thousand suicides? I couldn't wrap my brain around it.

Why did a thousand people commit suicide inside the ship, Suski? Why were they all stabbed in the stomach before they killed themselves?

Suski looked at me from across the table. There was something in his eyes. It wasn't just stoic staring. There was hurt in there. Or maybe I was projecting that on to him, seeing what I wanted to see. I met his gaze and held it, but below the table my hand began to shake.

What had happened on that ship in the week that it was sitting in the dirt by Lakeville? What were they afraid of?

Was it a fight? The losers got stabbed in the stomach?

I glanced up at Suski. He was on the winning team. Was he a good guy or a bad guy?

TEN

I hadn't been sure how to explain it to Coya, that we were going to investigate her home. But she was up in the library watching a video for history class.

Rachel and Brynne hadn't seen the ship in real life and were completely awed by it even in the waning evening light. The National Guard officer at the entrance to the site was considerably less awed by us. He looked at all of our IDs, and even though our names were on the list, he called my dad and asked if we were really the Alice, Brynne, and Rachel that he was waiting for. Dad confirmed our identities and confirmed the identity of Bluebell, and soon we were heading down a hardpacked dirt road away from I-35 and toward the enormous object that was blocking out all the skyline. The guardsman had hung a tag on my rearview mirror—a big green 16—and as we drove, traffic directors motioned me to take this road and then that road, and we got closer and closer to the ship.

It was completely overwhelming. I had been to the Grand Canyon once and had been stunned by the size of that—that something could be so incredibly massive, it stretched from horizon to horizon. This spaceship felt a little like that. It was an enormous wall of darkness that rose higher than I could see and in both directions away from us. In fact, at one point Rachel pointed up through the sunroof and said that it was above us; we were under the curve of the cylinder.

One more guard guided us toward a parking lot that contained about eighty cars and a dozen large tents.

"Do you think we're going to see more aliens?" Brynne asked.

"I don't know," I said, pulling into an empty spot. "Dad said he was working with alien engineers. But I think they'll just be like Coya and Suski."

I dialed Dad's cell, and he answered quickly. "You're ten minutes late."

"I didn't want to get pulled over and miss this completely."

"Good. You're in the parking lot? Wait—I see you."

A moment later he was at my car shaking Brynne and Rachel's hands again and generally acting like he was powered by coffee and excitement.

"Did you sleep last night?" I asked.

"Sleep is for the weak," he said, motioning us toward one of the tents.

"You can't have a heart attack and leave me an orphan. You know I'd just blow all our money on drugs and rock 'n' roll."

"All the best heroes are orphans," Dad said. "You'd be in good company, if you went on a quest or something." He looked at the other girls. "You're not orphans, are you?"

"Not me," they both answered.

"You'll never amount to anything. Anyway, here's the deal. You're going to get suited up. I'm going to give you a pad of stickers that have numbers on them. We're going to go through the ship, find rooms that haven't been touched, and take pictures of them. Treat it like a crime scene—don't touch anything, just take pictures, and one of these numbered stickers needs to be in every shot. Every room has a number, and every picture from that room uses the same number. Clear as mud?"

We nodded.

"We're exploring places in the ship where no one has gone?" I asked. "You're sure this isn't dangerous? What if we find another . . . you know." I still hadn't told the girls about the suicides. I don't know why. I just hoped it wouldn't come up.

"That's why you'll have your big strong father with you," he said. "I work for NASA, you know."

We entered the tent. It was brightly lit, with shower stalls lining every wall.

"We're taking showers?"

"When you come out of the ship," he said. "Just a precaution. Decontamination."

"What about our clothes?"

He walked to a row of shelves and pulled down bundles. "Hospital scrubs. Now, go change."

After we changed, we climbed the ten stories to the top of the scaffolding, wearing bulky safety glasses, latex gloves, and hard hats with chin straps.

"I can't believe we're doing this," Rachel said, her camera swinging around her neck on its strap.

"It's going to be a short climb down once we get inside," Dad said, shouting to be heard over the cold October wind. "You have to remember that the entire ship is curved in a big circle. When the ship was in motion, rotating, you could jog around the inside of the cylinder—all the way around the ship until you got back to the same place."

"Just like *2001*," Rachel said.

Dad turned back to look at me. "Someone knows good culture."

"Rachel's one of those show-off kids," I said, and she turned and grinned at me.

"The point is," Dad continued, "we're going to have to climb back down with ropes, to a place where it's flatter.

Don't worry—it's not that steep. I assume none of you are afraid of heights or you wouldn't be standing up here on this scaffolding."

"Dad?" I asked. "Are there aliens inside?"

"A few," he said. "But we probably won't see them. They've gone with some of the more technical teams to check out the engines."

We reached the top of the scaffold, and the door that we knew so well from TV. I stopped and turned, looking out at the mass of tents and army vehicles. The sun was setting, leaving a few beautiful strands of orange and pink before it dropped behind the horizon. I tried to imagine what it looked like in the morning, or at night. This was the aliens' first view of our world—their first view of what their new life would be like.

It looked scary.

"Here," Dad said, shoving something into my hand. I took it and held it up. A breathing mask—not just a little flimsy paper one, like the kind they had handed out to the aliens on the ground, but a big one, like a gas mask. It was heavy, and I pulled it over my head awkwardly, watching Rachel and Brynne do the same with theirs. Dad helped us tighten the straps and get them in place.

"Okay," he said. "This is it. Are you ready?"

I had butterflies in my stomach—giant, alien butterflies with extra wings and bad attitudes.

Rachel was already nodding, and I heard her muffled "Yes." Brynne followed suit. So I pretended I was courageous, and I stepped forward and was glad I had a mask covering most of my face.

Dad led us to the door. There were large halogen lights set up, flooding the hallway with light.

I didn't see any of the ship's lights—maybe the walls glowed or something when the ship was running. This "door" was a hole in the floor of the corridor. The hull was more than a foot thick, and we could see the jagged marks of whatever cutting tool the aliens had used to get through.

It wasn't as steep as I had expected, looking down the hall—maybe a ten-degree downward slope. There were several nylon ropes running from somewhere above us. Dad instructed us to grab a rope and start heading down, but I was too in awe of the spaceship, of crossing the threshold. The walls were all some kind of silvery plastic something. It appeared that they'd once been gleaming and shiny, but the handprints of fifty-five thousand people had turned them into a smudgy mess.

Fifty-five thousand *aliens*.

Dad led the way, holding on to one of the ropes at about waist height and walking down the slope. Rachel followed after, and then Brynne, and then me. It felt a little bit like the county fair funhouses that we went to when I was a little kid, where the floors weren't straight and you couldn't keep your balance without a hand on the wall the whole time. There were numbered stickers everywhere, sloppily applied by the first photographers who had taken pictures of this hallway.

"Is all the power off?" I tried to shout through my massive filter.

Dad looked back. "There is some power still on in other parts of the ship—there are still life-support systems running, heating and air flow. In some places the lights work, but not here. All of that is up toward the front of the ship. It's one of the mysteries, because back here is where most of the people lived, as you'll soon see."

Before long, the curve of the ship got flatter, and we didn't need the ropes to help us descend. I dropped mine and let my hand skim the wall. It was smooth, and my latex glove slid across it easily. Every twenty or thirty feet there was a thick ring protruding from the floor. They made convenient places to hang utility lights.

"What are these rings for?" I called to Dad.

"We don't know," he said with a shrug.

"Haven't you asked the aliens?"

"Not a priority yet. Bigger fish to fry. But my guess is that they're some kind of tether for when the ship is in zero gravity. When it's not spinning. They've been really useful for our guys who are climbing into the hard-to-reach spots. The rings are all over the place. Every room, every hall."

We reached a point where the ground was almost level,

and a long hallway extended to our left, toward the front of the ship. Most of the electrical cables headed that way, and that was where we went.

"These marks," Dad said, pointing to a big red sticker next to a door, "mean that a room has been photographed. We'll keep going until we reach a room that hasn't."

All of the rooms with red dots were dark, no one bothering to light them now that pictures had been taken.

The spaceship definitely didn't look like something out of *Star Trek*. It was too dirty, too cluttered. Too lived-in. There was debris scattered all along this corridor—blankets and wrappings and plastic containers and shreds of clothing. I couldn't imagine what it must have been like down here for the last four or five days as fifty-five thousand aliens, many of whom were wounded, waited in the dark for their turn to leave.

But it wouldn't have been dark, would it? They'd have had flashlights and glowing orbs and magic crazy alien lights. They were the Guides, after all. They were here to teach us a better way of life, and that meant that they couldn't have suffered too much. They had to have taken care of themselves somehow.

We walked for what felt like half an hour until we finally reached a door that wasn't marked.

"Here we go," Dad said. He turned on a lantern and led us into the room.

It was wide and square, with rows of what looked like countertops—like it was a lab of some kind. On the far side was a long row of tall, thin cabinets.

"Okay," he said. "Remember, long shots and close-ups. And make sure one of these number stickers is in every shot. This room is number . . ." —he pulled off the top sticker—"2139. So make sure the number 2139 is in every—"

His phone rang. (The Velvet Underground. I'd picked it out for him.) He talked for thirty seconds, but I could tell he was leaving.

"I'm sorry, girls, but I need to be elsewhere." We all began to protest but he held up his phone. "Don't worry. This is easy work: sticker, point, and click. You can do it. I'm not going far. If you need me for any reason, you can call me. This ship gets amazingly good reception. Like it was made for it or something."

"Do we open doors?" Brynne asked, looking at the cabinets on the far wall, which suddenly seemed more ominous.

"Yeah," he said, "but keep your bearings in mind. Everything on that wall is tilting in toward us slightly, so it might come falling out."

"And NASA is cool with us letting stuff fall and break?" I asked.

"Ideally, you won't let anything break," he said. "But mistakes happen, and we're severely understaffed and trying to get this ship inspected and documented ASAP. Open the cupboards slowly, and try not to let anything fall."

"What if there are jars with alien life forms in there?" Brynne asked, and I couldn't tell whether she was scared or hopeful. "What if we stumble onto a bug collection?"

"First," he said, "everything in this ship has already crashed at six hundred miles an hour. So, anything fragile has already broken. Second, if there's a bug collection, take a bunch of pictures before everything gets away." He smiled at that.

"Are you sure you work for NASA?" Brynne said. "And you're not just Alice's big brother?"

"He's my dad," I said. "He's always like this."

"Seriously, girls," he said. "We don't know how long we'll have access to this ship. We don't know if the Guides are going to seize it back in negotiations and live in it, or what. And we don't know whether the UN is going to send in its own inspectors and take the project over. I wouldn't have asked you to come if we didn't desperately need manpower."

That answer seemed to pacify everyone, including me, although now I had the heebie-jeebies about alien bugs.

"How far do we go?" I asked, as he moved toward the door, leaving the lantern in the room for us.

"As far and as long as you're willing to stay. Are you girls okay?"

We all nodded, our big gas masks bobbing heavily on our faces.

"Then I'm going to go," he said. "Love you, Aly."

"You, too."

We spent half an hour in the first room and probably took a couple hundred pictures. For a room that looked like a lab, there was hardly anything in the drawers. We found that they opened in a rather high-tech fashion—with a little push, they'd pop out slowly, almost like they were automated. But there wasn't power on in this room, so it must have been some kind of pneumatics. Rachel said she'd seen similar drawers before and they weren't an example of amazing alien technology, but I was still impressed.

The tall, skinny cabinets had tools in them that looked like farm instruments. Long sticks with hooks, loops, or spikes on the ends. There didn't seem to be anything special about them except that the sticks looked well worn, like they'd been used a lot over a long period of time. I couldn't figure out what the aliens would have done with them, though.

Aside from that, the only other unusual thing in the room was that the ceiling was high—I'd noticed that in the hallway, too. If I were designing a spaceship, it would be more economic on space, with ceilings that barely fit me. But maybe this ship was like my BMW—all about comfort. Maybe that was why there were only fifty-five thousand aliens on board, instead of a hundred thirty thousand.

Rachel took the lantern and we left the room. Brynne turned and put a big red dot next to the door.

"I know this is totally off subject," Brynne said as we walked to the next room, "but scrubs have got to be the most comfortable clothes ever."

Rachel and I laughed.

"Seriously," Brynne said, picking her way around debris on the floor. "These are way better than my pajamas. I'm going to get rid of flannel and stick with these."

We turned a corner at the next doorway and shone the light in.

Rachel gasped.

It wasn't hard to identify this room. There were five rows of beds between the floor and ceiling, with the thinnest mattresses I'd ever seen. There was maybe two feet of space between each bed and the bed above it—maybe. It was probably less.

I grabbed on to one of the hard metal rings next to the door and wondered what kind of smells would be assaulting us if we didn't have our filters on. The room was a mess—like what I imagined the boys' dorm to be like, but worse.

Brynne pulled out a sticker and slapped it on the nearest object—the end of a bed. It said 2140. She took a wide shot of the room, but couldn't get a fair representation of the distance—this place seemed to stretch far down the length of the ship, running parallel to the main hallway. We knew there wouldn't be enough stickers for this room, so we just folded our sticker tablets like A-frames, placing them on each bed and taking pictures. There were no drawers here and no sign of bathrooms. It made me wonder how this place worked, and why on Earth—why in the galaxy—these aliens thought they had a prayer of being our Guides.

We moved farther into the room, setting up our shots and clearing row after row of the beds. Rachel found a dark spot on the floor, which totally paralyzed her, and Brynne knelt down beside it and tilted the lantern close.

"Is it blood?" Rachel asked. Her face looked green even in the yellowish light from the lantern.

"I think so," Brynne said. "I bet an alien was sleeping in bed when the ship crashed, and they split their head open."

"So, guys," I said, taking a deep breath. "My dad said that deep in the ship they found a room where a thousand of the Guides had committed mass suicide."

There was a long pause. "Whoa. Why?" Brynne asked.

"He doesn't know the answer. They all had been stabbed in the stomach, and then they'd slit their throats, or something like that."

"We need to ask Suski what happened," Rachel said firmly. "Even if they were injured, they must have good doctors. I mean, they mastered interstellar travel."

"I'm not so sure I'd say 'mastered,'" I replied. "If the Olympics have taught me nothing else, it's that you've got to stick the landing. I'd say these Guide gymnasts fell right on their butts and started to cry in front of the judges."

We moved past the blood stain and onto the next bank of beds. There was nothing out of the ordinary here, or so I thought.

"Uh, guys?" Brynne asked. "Does this fall under our jurisdiction?"

In between this bank of beds and the next was a ladder leading up through a hole in the ceiling.

Rachel and Brynne both looked at me, as though NASA authority was passed on through the genes. I stared up at the hole. It was completely dark up there, and it looked like a claustrophobic fit.

"Well," I said, trying to gather my courage. "If we go up there and it connects to another hallway, then it's that hallway's problem. But if it only connects to this room, then it's our problem." I paused, then took a deep breath. "And I'm going to go first, because I'm frigging Wonder Woman."

Brynne handed me the lantern, and I could see the smile in her eyes. "Here's your lasso of truth."

"Wonder Damn Woman," I said, moving to the ladder and placing a foot on the rung. It was perfectly strong, and I took a deep breath.

"We'll be sure to tell the boys," Rachel said.

"At your funeral," Brynne said. "Well, memorial service. I don't think there will be a body."

I climbed the ladder, and before long, even my face filter couldn't block out the smell. I knew what this room was before I lifted the lantern through the hole and took a look.

"The good news," I shouted down, "is that I don't see any monsters. The bad news is that this is a very overused bathroom, and there are no doors leading to another hallway. So it's all us."

There were space toilets, not unlike the kind I'd seen on the space shuttle simulators in museums my dad had taken me to. They were designed to operate in zero gravity, using a very unpleasant suction technology. When the ship wasn't working anymore and the power in this area was turned off, people continued to use the toilets, but nothing was sucking.

Well, it all sucked. It stunk, and I didn't want to touch anything, not to affix stickers or to set down the lantern. The light wasn't good enough to tell what was filthy and what wasn't, but I assumed everything was.

The job got a little better as we moved past the long row of toilets and got to a long row of showers. These were a little different from the suction power of the toilets. It looked like water actually poured down on people in sealed chambers.

I recoiled from one that appeared to have been turned into a toilet, but Brynne said it looked more like blood, and luckily she was happy to use her stickers in order to take a dozen shots of the bloody *Psycho* shower stall. After half an hour in the feces-filled room, we all were eager to make our escape back down the ladder and into the relative peace of the messy room below.

We continued through the room, photographing row after row of beds. By my count we passed more than two hundred fifty rows of them—maybe three hundred. The venture up the ladder had made me lose count.

There was some kind of writing on the wall, on each bed. Maybe it was art like Coya and Suski had claimed, but it looked like the kind of symbols I'd seen outside.

"I'm never going to get this smell out of my hair," Brynne said. "I can tell."

"I can't smell much through the mask," Rachel said.

"Neither can I," Brynne said, "but I just know it. We're all doomed to smell like alien poo for days."

"You're the one who got excited about the blood," I said.

"Blood is . . . scientific," Brynne said. "Blood is interesting. Blood doesn't smell like an outhouse."

"Hate to say it," I said. "But we've got another one."

"Another bathroom?"

"Nope," I said, and moved between two banks of beds. There was a door that looked jammed, like it had been a powered entrance that had been forced open.

The lantern was shoved into my hand again. "Lasso of truth," Brynne said.

"Wonder Woman isn't the only superheroine," I said.

"You can be Supergirl. You'd be just like her—blond, big boobs, short skirt."

"Flattery will get you nowhere."

"What about you, Rachel?" I asked. "Black Widow had red hair. Supertight bodysuit. Got with Jeremy Renner."

There was a smile in Rachel's voice. "I'm going to decide that I'm offended you didn't accuse me of having big boobs."

I looked down at the lantern. "Lasso of truth. That seems like a stupid weapon. Why not a machine gun of truth?" I held the lantern up to the door and saw that there were a few glowing lights inside. So this side of the ship wasn't completely without power. I stepped across the threshold, Rachel and Brynne on my heels.

There was blood everywhere. And worse, those farm tools we'd seen in the other room—the lab—were here, too. They were covered in blood, their spikes and hooks crusted with it. I think I would have thrown up if I hadn't been wearing a mask. I didn't dare take it off to throw up, and I certainly wasn't going to throw up with it on. Rachel pivoted around and stepped back out of the room.

"Okay," I said, turning and facing a wall so I wouldn't have to look at the mess all across the floor. There was more than just blood. There was . . . flesh. Matter. Whatever word is used for little bits of bodies.

"Okay," Brynne said quietly.

"Let's just take pictures and get out of here."

"Okay."

I slapped a sticker—2142—on the nearest thing, a bed. There were six beds in this room—bigger and nicer, with blood-soaked mattresses. I started snapping pictures, shaking as I tried to hold the camera still.

"It could have been an accident," Brynne said. "The aliens in here could have died in the crash. And then the farm tools were used to pry the door open. Right?"

"Right," I said, "an accident. Lots of blood, but there are lots of sharp corners in this room. Lots of places for a person—for an alien—to crash into. Frankly, I'm amazed we haven't seen more bloody messes all over this sleeping area. People should have gotten thrown all over."

"Why aren't you guys calling it what it is?" Rachel said, plainly trembling. "Another mass suicide."

"There's so much blood," Brynne said, but it wasn't scientist Brynne talking. It was teenager, only-a-few-years-ago-was-a-little-kid Brynne talking.

"We did see a few wounded aliens leaving the ship," I said, trying to be optimistic.

"I hate to burst your bubble," Brynne said, trying to shake off her nerves and go back to being the scientist. "But these people didn't survive. People don't have this much blood in them. Not enough to lose this much and survive. I don't care what your high-tech alien rescue equipment is. These people didn't make it. These people didn't even leave the room to get to where the other people committed suicide. They died right here."

"If they're like humans," I said. "You called them people, which they're not."

"Maybe," Brynne said.

We continued through the room, stepping over blood where we could and tiptoeing across it where we couldn't. We affixed stickers and took pictures, and it was horrifying. It was like the Halloween decor at the dorms if all the fake blood and gore were real. It was a horror movie.

When we'd taken pictures of room 2142 from every angle we could think of, we moved back into the long room with bunk beds.

I could tell I was breathing too fast, and Brynne was bent in half, hands on her knees. Rachel leaned against a wall, hugging herself.

I pulled out my phone. Dad answered on the fourth ring.

"Find anything awesome?" he asked.

"Dad," I said. "This place is a nightmare. I think we just found a murder scene. Like a real, live murder scene. Or another suicide. We don't know."

"Aly," he said, and I heard him mumble something to someone else. "Aly, I'm sorry."

"We're done, Dad. Sorry, but this ship is crazy."

"That's okay," he said. "What did you find?"

"A murder room. A haunted house. I don't know what it was."

"I'm like half a mile away from you now. Can you wait there?"

"Yeah," I said. "If you can hurry."

"Okay. Remember, if you need to leave just follow those metal rings and the extension cords the way you came in. Seriously, honey, don't worry about it. You did great."

I was starting to cry. "We only got four rooms."

"That's four we didn't have before," he said. "Listen, I'm coming. We'll figure this out."

"Okay."

"You all right?"

"I guess."

It took him seven minutes to get there. I was counting. None of us said anything. No speculation, no jokes to lighten the mood. Just fear.

These were *Guides*. But what the hell were they going to be guiding us about?

Dad saw us sitting, nervous and frightened, on the beds opposite the door to the murder room. He pointed at the jammed door without saying a word. I nodded.

He aimed his flashlight into the room for ten or twenty seconds, and then squeezed inside. He was in there for a good five minutes before he called out: "Did you get photos of this whole place?"

“Yeah,” I answered, finally standing up and walking back to the door.

“We haven’t found anything like this anywhere else. We thought the suicide room was the only place like this.”

I started to speak, but my flashlight caught a torn piece of flesh, and I had to fight to keep from throwing up.

“I’m sorry, Alice.”

I closed my eyes. “It’s okay.”

“No. I’m really sorry.”

“We’re leaving.”

“That’s a good idea. I’ll come with you.” He got on his radio and called back to someone, telling them he’d be back in thirty minutes. He slid back through the jammed door and gave me a hug, and I wanted to cry, but I stopped myself. I had to be tougher than that. For Dad.

ELEVEN

All I could think about was Coya. She was the gentlest creature I think I'd ever met. So calm and fragile. And she had been stranded inside the ship for so long.

"Dad," I asked, holding his hand like I was half my age. Wishing I still was. "Did they still have lights on inside the ship? While they waited to open the door?"

"We think so, Aly. At least most of the time."

"Good."

We showered for a long time at the NASA tent, and then when we got back home, we showered again, hoping that by some miracle our shampoos and bodywashes would somehow soak through our skulls and into our brains and turn us back into innocent teenage girls.

When we got back to our room, Brynne asked if she

could sleep in the room with me and Rachel—it was late and she didn't want to be alone in her room with Coya. Not tonight.

"Tell me what you're thinking," I said, knowing that this was exactly what the stupid RAs would have wanted me to ask. They'd be all into us expressing our feelings in order to process what happened.

"It's not like movies," Rachel said. "Well, it's not like most movies. It's like *Alien*. It's not like *2001*."

"These people are not Guides," Brynne said. "I don't care what they say. I don't care how miserable it was waiting inside a spaceship for everyone to get out. They don't have some heretofore undiscovered miraculous philosophy. They're people who can't even be bothered to make their beds. I can understand a messy bathroom, because they didn't have running water, but not making their beds? Not cleaning up the hallway? I know that's petty, but I don't care. Did you guys see that movie with Keanu Reeves where he's an alien who comes to tell the world how we've all gotten it wrong? It's *The Day the Earth Stood Still* or something like that. Anyway, his solution is to wipe everything out and make the world start over from the cavemen. Maybe that's the kind of Guides these aliens are. They're not peaceful. They're messy, and they're ready to start a fight."

"I'll admit it," Rachel said. "I'm a *Star Wars* nerd. I love it. And the production designers say they want to give their ships a 'lived-in' look. But they don't have ships like that. The real world sucks."

"I'm sorry," I said, staring at the ceiling. The textured paint reminded me of a sea of stars. "I'm sorry I dragged you into this. I should have warned you about the suicides."

"No," Rachel said, leaning up on one elbow. "It was awesome. It was horrible, and I hated it, but it was going into a spaceship just days after it landed. If I was with a group of NASA researchers—people who knew what they should have done when they came across what we found—then I'd go back in a heartbeat."

"You would? Seriously?" Brynne said.

"Yes, seriously. It was totally a freak show, but that's because it was just the three of us, and we didn't have any real protection other than the lasso of truth. But if there were a dozen of us, and one of us was your dad, and he knew what he was doing and he was the one who entered all the rooms first, then I'd go back. I just want someone who knows what they're doing to be the one to discover the horrible stuff and tell me that it's okay."

"I think I'm with you," I said, and Brynne sighed. "No, really. I'd go back with someone who had a gun."

"I don't need a gun," Rachel said. "Just someone who could talk about all the bad stuff and explain to us why we're not looking at a mass murder."

Brynne sat up. "But what if it *was* a mass murder?"

"It wasn't," Rachel said. "It was a ship crashing at six hundred miles an hour. I don't know why those pointy sticks were in the room, but they were an accident waiting to happen. In low gravity they probably never even got looked at twice."

"So," Brynne said. "We just have to find out what those pointy sticks were for. Because I can't see much reason for them other than to kill someone."

"They have to have some other purpose," I said. "Because killing people doesn't seem like the point of the ship. What ship crosses the galaxy and along the way kills half the people on board?"

I swung my legs over the end of the bed and stood up. I was wearing a clean pair of scrubs. We all were—they were the best part of our trip to the spaceship. We didn't want to leave without a souvenir.

"Where are you going?" Rachel asked.

"Coya's in the other room. Let's just ask her. It's what Wonder Woman would do, right?"

Brynne and Rachel grimaced, then nodded. We trooped into the next room. Coya was sleeping, and we softly called her name until she sat up and looked at us. I motioned for her to put on her translator, and she did.

"So," I said. "We have a question."

"Yes?" Coya said.

"We went inside your ship."

She nodded slowly, looking confused.

"We found a room while we were there. There were tools—hooks and spikes on long poles."

What tiny amount of color she had in her face vanished.

"Do you know what those hooks and spikes are for?" I asked her.

She suddenly took a great interest in smoothing out her quilt, adamantly avoiding all eye contact.

"Coya, honey," Brynne said. "Can you tell us what those were for?"

"For working on the ship," she said. "We all worked on the ship. Some people used hooks and spikes."

"To do what?" I asked.

"I don't know. It was not my job."

"What was your job?"

"I had many jobs," she said, seeming eager to change the subject. "I cleaned. There is a lot that needs to be cleaned on a ship so big. I also worked in a laboratory. I was learning how to extract blood and test it."

"Test it for what?" Brynne asked, her tone changing to one of academic interest.

"Purity. There were sicknesses on the ship. I do not know how it worked. I was only a beginner."

"I have to ask you a hard question," I said. "And I don't want to upset you."

She looked me, her expression wary.

"When we were in the ship, we found a room where there was blood all over the floor."

"No," Coya said adamantly.

"Coya," I said. "It looked like people had been murdered there. Do you know what murder is?"

"You mean killing a person?"

"Yes."

"There were no murders."

"Do you know about a room like that?"

"Many people were hurt in the crash," she said. "It may be their blood."

"Were people killed in the crash?"

She paused for a long time, looking from Brynne, to Rachel, to me. "Yes. People were killed in the crash."

"Where are their bodies?"

"Why are you asking me this?"

"Because we're worried," Rachel said.

"Worried that I will kill you?" Coya said with sudden outrage. "I am not like that. I am not a monster."

"We're not saying you're a monster," I said. "We just want to know what happened, so we can help. We're worried about you."

"You don't need to be worried about me. Not anymore."

"But—" I began.

"I'm tired now," Coya interrupted. "Good night."

"We're your friends," I pleaded. "We want to help." But

it was clear we had worn out our welcome for the night. Rachel shrugged, and the three of us tiptoed out of the room.

Brynne slept in Rachel's bed, neither one of them snoring, which made me feel bad because I knew that I did. But I just couldn't sleep. What was the aliens' plan? They weren't good at landing their ship, and they didn't even have a real door for coming out. Was this really the plan of aliens who wanted to guide us? To crash-land and fill us with terror for two weeks while we fed them and gave them shelter and warmth? Were they beggars, come to teach us the true meaning of Christmas?

"I'm going to find something to eat," I whispered, but neither Rachel nor Brynne made a sound.

Except I wasn't going to find something to eat. As soon as I got up, I texted Kurt to ask him to meet me in the main common room. I needed to talk to someone who hadn't been in the ship, who hadn't seen what we'd seen.

I crept past Coya's room and stepped out into the hallway. The lights were on halfway, but the dimness didn't scare me. This part of the school was too new to look creepy.

I passed the cafeteria and made it to the common room. It was the first time I had been there when the TV was off. I checked my phone. It was three in the morning. We had class in five hours, and I hadn't slept a wink. Kurt wasn't there yet, so I went to the cafeteria and got myself a Diet Coke.

By the time I got back to the common room, Kurt had turned on the gas fireplace and was shoving a couch up close to it. When he saw me, he smiled. He looked different without his glasses.

"Don't get any ideas, hot shot," I said. "I dragged you out of bed to tell you horror stories, not to woo you with midnight fantasies."

"The only ideas I'm getting are that my feet are freezing," he said.

"You are such a liar," I said. "Just know that any ideas you have that would result in me spilling my Diet Coke are bad ones."

I sat down on the couch—an orange modern thing that was really beautiful but could have been more comfortable. I leaned back and put my stocking feet up on the hearth. Kurt sat next to me. He was wearing a long-sleeve T-shirt and flannel pajama pants, and he put his bare feet next to mine. What we really needed was a big blanket.

Because it was Minnesota at three a.m. Get your mind out of the gutter.

"First of all," I said, "you have to tell me that I can trust you."

"Implicitly."

"I need more than that. I need . . . an embarrassing story," I said. "Blackmail material."

"What magnitude of embarrassing story are we talking

about? I mean, I don't want to tell you something extremely embarrassing in exchange for something only mild in return."

"We went in the spaceship," I said.

His mouth hung open for a minute. "Who's 'we'?"

"Me, Brynne, and Rachel. With my dad. So, big-time embarrassing."

"Wow. I don't know if I have something that level of embarrassing."

"Do the best you can."

"Seventh grade," he said, and paused.

"This already sounds promising."

"My first year in a coed boarding school. We had it in our heads that the funniest thing in the world was to hide somewhere and get accidentally discovered. So, like, you'd hide in the closet for hours, and then someone would come by and open the door and you'd scare the crap out of them."

"I'd say this sounds like seventh-grade-level embarrassing."

"It wasn't just the boys. The girls did it, too. Anyway, I was trying to be the best at it, because whoever created the biggest scare got popularity points. It was very competitive. Somehow I got into the girls' dorm, which was a lot harder in middle school."

I was already covering my face. I knew this couldn't end well.

"So I had it in my head that the funniest thing would be to get under a girl's bed, and when she came in, I'd grab her leg, and she'd scream, and everyone would laugh and I'd be a hero."

"Oh no."

"The problem was that I got in the room and under the bed, but she came in too soon, and I was facing the wrong way, so she was sitting on her bed before I could do anything."

I could feel my face turning red on his behalf, although he was plenty red himself. "And?"

"And I lay under the bed for an hour, terrified, trying to figure out the best way to get myself out of the situation. Finally I just said, 'Boo.' I spent the rest of middle school as 'That Kid Who Hid Under a Girl's Bed and Watched Her Undress.'"

"Ouch."

"It was not my finest hour."

"Okay, that works," I said. "It might even be worse than anything I'm going to tell you."

Then I laid it all out for him. I told him about the lab, the long rows of beds, the awful bathroom, and the murder room. I knew Rachel didn't think it was a mass murder, but I couldn't believe it was an accident. It didn't look like people had been thrown around the room in the crash.

There weren't any bodies, though. Maybe they were brought out with the wounded.

I started crying. I was so overwhelmed.

And because I was crying, Kurt had to be a gentleman and

hold my hand, and then I had to lean my shoulder against his, and soon my Diet Coke was sitting on the hearth, because it was hard to hug him with only one arm. He hugged me back, and I cried like a freaking idiot, and he nestled his face into my hair.

Eventually I fell asleep with my cheek against his chest. He woke me when the sun was peeking in the windows. I don't know if he slept at all, but I hadn't slept that well since the ship had crashed into Earth and changed all of our lives.

TWELVE

It was the next day that Brynne dropped the bomb.

We hadn't seen her all day. And I admit, I had too much on my mind to notice her absence. It was during dinner that she texted Rachel and me and told us to hurry to the room. When we arrived, Emily Fenton was there. Coya wasn't.

"You're going to want to sit down for this," Brynne said.

Rachel and I exchanged looks, but obeyed quickly. "That's what they tell people on TV. Does it really matter?"

Brynne ignored me. She could hardly stand still. "Okay, this is crazy. Remember how I took the cheek swab DNA sample from Coya? I know this is batcrap crazy, but I've run the test twice from her cheek swab and twice from her hair—I helped brush her hair and pulled a couple strands. Terrible, I know. Anyway, she's human."

"What?" Rachel asked. "But she's an alien."

"Nope," Brynne said, shaking her head. "Well, I don't know how 'alien' is defined. But biologically Coya is a human. And I can't be the only person who's figured this out. The government must know about it. I bet they're hiding it so that we don't freak out. But that's not the weirdest part."

"How could she be human?" Rachel asked.

"Hold on," she said, with a smile. She held up her hand, but it was shaking. "This all fits together. And I know it sounds crazy, but just follow me."

Rachel, sitting on her bed, pulled a pillow to her chest and hugged it.

Brynne smiled. "I figured out the human thing five days ago—sorry I didn't tell you—I was testing and retesting—and I've been trying to nail down Coya's genetic ancestry since then. I wanted to know where the Guides came from. So I went to Emily, and she told me where to look. The answer's crazy."

She paused and took a breath.

"Well?" I prompted. I turned to Emily. "You're the language Bruner. Please don't tell me they're all speaking pig latin and we missed it."

Emily smiled. "Once Brynne told me they were human, I had something to work with. I went with a digital recorder and made a list of words, and well, it's not as easy to figure out as something like DNA. DNA doesn't change a lot over five hundred years. But language does. There are tools online to just identify a language, but not one that's degraded."

"What do you mean by 'degraded'?" Rachel asked.

Emily brushed some loose strands of hair from her face. "Think about Britain. They have a lot of accents there, but compare them to America—we're totally different. And Australia: they're completely different, too. We all started out in the same place, but we've all evolved differently."

"Oh," Rachel said. "And how Canada says *sorry* weird."

"Yeah."

"Can we get on with it?" I asked, grabbing Emily's arm and shaking her. "What did you find out?"

"They're speaking a really bastardized version of Keresan."

I opened my mouth to speak, but nothing came out.

"What's Keresan?" Rachel asked.

I could barely talk. "Um . . . Keresan is a language spoken by half a dozen tribes in New Mexico. They're all Pueblo tribes. Acoma, Laguna—those are the ones I've been to. There are others to the east."

"The language has really morphed over the years," Emily put in.

Brynne spoke. "And the DNA databases I've searched say they're not any one of those tribes, but they have the markers for being an older tribe that those tribes are descended from. I need to do more research."

"What could it be?" Rachel asked.

I sighed. "The language is like a puebloan nation, but not. And the DNA is like a puebloan nation, but not. Are we talking about the Anasazi here?"

"That's what I think," Brynne said.

Rachel asked the big question. "What are the Anasazi?"

Brynne pointed to me and finally sat down. I spoke. "They're a tribe that was huge in the Four Corners area from about the seventh century to the fourteenth. It's kind of amazing how we don't all know about them here in America—they were huge. They built giant buildings, four stories tall, and roads that went perfectly straight for a hundred miles. Have you heard of Mesa Verde? The Cliff Palace?"

Rachel straightened up. "I do remember that!" She pulled out her tablet and flipped through the pictures until she found one on *National Geographic*'s site and held it up. A mortar-and-stone dwelling was built into the alcove of a cliff.

"So why them?" Brynne asked. "And why did they move out of these awesome cliff houses to the deserty south? I've looked up Laguna and Acoma, and there's not a tree to be seen."

"Well, first, they moved to the cliffs because they were afraid of something. Admittedly, that's a theory. There's no evidence of warfare. But they left their great civilization in the south—Chaco Canyon—and moved up to these highly defensible cliffs. They had watchtowers and hidden entrances and everything you'd need to stop people from getting you. So they came afraid. And then they just left and started up all the little pueblos."

Emily, who was leaning against the closet, spoke. "I read that Anasazi isn't the real name for them anymore. We're supposed to call them Ancestral Puebloans."

All of us were quiet for a long minute.

"So," Rachel said. "To sum things up: we know the Guides are human, and we know that they're speaking Keresan—did I pronounce that right?" Emily nodded. "So we're assuming that, given the evolutionary changes to their language, they've been on that ship a long freaking time. Therefore, they're Anasazi, or Ancestral Puebloans. Am I getting that right?"

"Right," Brynne said, and bit her lip.

"Why are they so white? Or is that a racist question?" Rachel asked—she looked beet red.

"I don't know if it's racist, and *I'm* a Navajo."

Brynne leaned against the wall. "They've been on that ship for so long that their skin evolved to be white—they never saw the sun."

"Yeah," I said. "My dad told me. Like salamanders who live in caves. They're complete albinos because they never see UV light."

"I've heard of Mesa Verde," Rachel said. "What's Chaco Canyon?"

"No one goes to Chaco Canyon because it's an awful muddy, rutted road to get out there," I said. "But it's like one of the wonders of the world. Huge pueblos and roads and"—I looked at Brynne, who was nodding—"and astronomy stuff, amazing astronomy stuff.

"Maybe they got scared when a spaceship showed up and invited them aboard? I mean, I'm no *Ancient Aliens* TV show watcher. The guy on that show wouldn't be believable even if he did have a normal haircut, but are we talking about a mass alien abduction a thousand years ago?"

"Either that," Brynne said, "or they built a spaceship. Both ideas are crazy, but one is a lot more plausible."

"We need to talk to Coya and Suski," I said firmly.

Our first opportunity should have been gym class the next day, but Suski appeared and took Coya by the arm, leading her away from us. It was as if he could tell we were on a mission to uncover secrets, and he didn't trust Coya not to tell us what we needed to know.

The two of them, wearing gym clothes that included long jogging pants—there was something about them and covering up their legs—ran along the track of the indoor gym. I changed into shorts and a tank top and found an exercise bike.

I was nearly a mile into my ride when Kurt climbed up on the bike next to mine. He wore shorts and a soccer jersey and he set a water bottle up in the cup holder.

"Mind if I join you?" he asked.

"Not at all," I said, puffing away. "To what do I owe the pleasure?"

"Do I need a reason?"

"Nope."

"Well, there is one." He started pedaling and adjusted the resistance.

"I hope it's good."

"Unfinished business," he said.

"Ah, that."

"There was this whole episode the other night. I was talking. You were talking. There was a fireplace involved."

"I remember."

"And then someone—I'm not going to name any names—fell asleep."

"I believe that someone was crying her eyes out. So, you know, romantic."

"Well, it wasn't romantic," he said. "I'll grant you that. It just had the potential to appear romantic. To the outside observer."

"Don't tell me people are beginning to talk."

"They're not beginning to talk," he said. "Not a word. That's what troubles me. It should be a big scandal. You're the new girl, the rebel, and there's no scandal. You're killing me, Goodwin."

"What do you propose?" I asked.

"Dinner," he said. "Tonight."

"Like a date?"

"Well," he said, a small bead of sweat dripping down his forehead. "Yes. Like a date, but we're stuck in the school building."

I couldn't help but smile. "I've got something planned after gym." I nodded my head toward the track. "I'm going to try to get some information out of stone-faced Suski over there. But after that, I'm all yours."

"It's a deal. Also, how are you not even breaking a sweat on that bike?"

"Girls don't sweat," I said. "We glow."

"You're not even glowing."

"It's all the ice cream I eat. Cools down the body. Seriously. You should try it."

"One day your metabolism is going to catch up with you."

"Did you suddenly become my seventy-year-old grandma?"

"Not the best way to ask a girl out?"

"You did better the first time," I said. "This date better be good, because I have some holy-crap-awesome secrets to tell you."

"Are we talking black tie?"

"Do I look like a black-tie girl?"

"No."

"What time?"

"I'll be in the common room wearing my prom dress around seven."

"Done."

After gym I showered and changed. Since I didn't have any more classes that day, I decided to wear something other than my uniform: a skirt and a white button-up top with a scarf tied stylishly around my neck. I knew I'd need a sweater eventually, but I was still overheated from my ride.

I grabbed my laptop and went to the cafeteria. Suski was in the same place he always was. Coya was with him, and she smiled when I sat down. This time he had a textbook in front of him—humanities—and he was flipping through the pages.

I sat down and pointed to one of the pictures. "I've been there. To Cairo. The one thing they never show in the pictures and the books is how dirty the city is. Trash everywhere."

"What do you want?" His tone wasn't argumentative. But his tone was set by a computer voice, so I didn't know how he really meant it.

"I want to ask you some questions," I said. I found the bookmark on Rachel's tablet and opened the picture of Mesa Verde.

He didn't give it a second glance, but I guess it was dozens of generations back from him, if his ancestors ever saw it at all. Coya looked at it for several seconds and smiled before handing it back to me.

He closed the book. "You've been asking Coya a lot of questions."

I looked him in the face. He reminded me of a white marble sculpture, like the pictures in the humanities textbook. Like Edward in the Twilight books (but not in the movies—*ew*). What? Can't a girl read a book about men sculpted out of marble?

"I have been asking a lot of questions," I said. "I bet a lot of people have been asking a lot of questions."

"You shouldn't have made her hair blue. She shouldn't be with you. She should be with her own kind. With me. Someone who can protect her."

"She is protected," I said. "She has me, and Rachel, and Brynne."

"We were told we would be protected, but only if we stayed inside the fence. I don't believe it."

"Here," I said, and stood up. "Come on."

He stood up, and I once again realized how massive this guy was. I don't know what his job on the ship had been, but it must have involved a lot of lifting.

"Try to attack me," I said.

He looked confused.

"Take off your microphone. I don't want to break it."

I moved toward him and unclipped the speaker and then reached out a hand for the headset. Very slowly and reluctantly he removed it.

"Come on," I said, waving him toward me. I was trying very hard to stand still, not in a ready stance.

He still didn't come, so I shoved him in the chest and then gestured, "Come on!"

Very slowly, like this was the dumbest thing he'd ever done, he stepped forward, arms stretched out before him. As soon as his hands touched my shirt, I swung my arms up through and around his, pinning his arms together. I reached my leg in for a sweep and pulled him forward, tripping him so he fell on his face.

From across the cafeteria, I heard cheers.

Suski looked stunned, and I reached out a hand to help him up. He took it and stood.

"Come on," I said again, and motioned him forward. My scarf was falling off, so I untied it and tossed it on the table.

He looked more determined now. He charged forward, wrapping me in a bear-hug tackle. I turned in his grip, putting my back to him, and used his forward momentum to toss him over my shoulder.

Sheesh, he was heavy. Must've been the chiseled marble.

We were attracting a crowd.

I reached down to help him up again, but he didn't take

my hand this time. He crouched into a more combative stance and swung one arm out to grab me. I caught his arm, wrapped it against my body, then flung my leg out against his waist, pinning him in a pain lock. He shouted something in his language. *"Eh-ya!"*

As much as I was enjoying getting to use my jujitsu again—and it helped that Suski didn't seem to know how to fight—he was a big guy, and even though I was winning, I was getting beat up. Short girls can only parry marble for so long, jujitsu or not. I pointed to his headset and speaker.

His stark white face was reddened with embarrassment as he clipped the device back on. I waved at all the people around us to go back to what they were doing.

"I was taking care of your sister," I said. "I wouldn't let anything happen to her."

He didn't respond, but picked up my scarf and handed it to me. I tied it loosely around my neck and then sat down.

"I like you guys," I said. "I want to take care of Coya. I just want you to talk to me."

"How did you do that?" he asked, rubbing his shoulder.

"It's called jujitsu. It's a way of fighting. I was trained to protect myself."

"I would like to learn," he said.

"I'll teach you," I said. "Tomorrow. And the next day. I can teach you a lot."

"What do you want to know?" He sat down across from me.

"I was in your spaceship," I said. "My dad works for the government."

He nodded.

"What was your job on the ship?"

"Why do you ask me these questions?" he asked sharply.

"I want to understand you," I said. "I *need* to understand all of your people."

"Many people don't want to understand," he said. "Many people just want to fight us. To kill us. That's why you have your guards in front of the school. I know this. Humans want to kill Coya and me."

"Not in this school," I said.

"No," he answered angrily. "Did you not hear the laughter when you hurt me? They want to see me hurt."

"That was because you're so big and I'm so small," I said, hoping I was right. "They were laughing at that. Not because you're a Guide."

"I do not know if I believe you."

I closed the laptop and sighed. "On the spaceship we found places where it looked like people were killed—places with a lot of blood. Do you know what happened?"

Coya answered, "We crashed. Many people were injured."

I nodded. "Yes, but we found other places where it looked

like people were murdered. We found weapons."

His lips were drawn into a thin, tight line. "If you found weapons, there must have been an accident during the crash."

"Where are the dead bodies?"

"These questions are painful," he said.

I didn't want to let him go, not when I was so close. "Where are the dead bodies?" I turned to Coya. "Do you know?"

Suski jumped in so Coya couldn't answer. "Whenever anyone dies on the ship, they get recycled. Their bodies are processed and used to feed the gardens."

I was repulsed, instantly and completely. I'd heard of human waste being used as fertilizer in Third World countries, but not processed corpses.

He must have seen the horror on my face, because he held out his hands. "Not the gardens for food. We have gardens that produce the air we breathe. When a man dies, his body is returned to the gardens to give the rest of us breath."

I relaxed slightly. "Processed."

"Yes," he said, as though it were the most normal thing in the world. Well, I guess it was for him. And I could see that it made some sense not to waste organic tissue—not to shoot a dead body into space. Still, the thought that Grandpa was getting mulched to feed a pool of algae was absolutely disgusting.

"One more question," I said, and he almost rolled his eyes. It seemed like he did the alien equivalent—some gesture with two fingers and a sigh.

I repeated the gesture—and the sigh. "Did I get that right?"

Suski almost smiled, but he pulled it back at the last minute. "What is your question?" he asked.

"Suski," I said, "and Coya." I was still stumbling over the question in my mind. I wanted the perfect segue, but nothing had come, or at least, nothing I'd seen.

"What?" Coya asked.

Might as well just ask it. I gripped the edge of the table, and then grabbed the arms of the chair, and finally just crossed my arms. "Do you know that you're not aliens? You're humans, just like us?"

Suski took a deep breath, held it, and then exhaled through his nose. Coya looked confused and waited for her brother to talk. "What makes you say that? We look different. Our language is different."

"There's a thing in our bodies—very, very small—called DNA. Brynne took a sample from Coya and—"

"When did she take a sample?" Coya asked, her face turning red.

"Remember when she rubbed that cotton swab on the inside of your cheek on the first day you got here?"

"What does it mean that we are humans?"

"I was hoping you could tell me."

"We don't know. Our people look like your people. That's just how it is."

"Here," I said, taking his humanities textbook from him and looking up the Anasazi. There were three pictures of pottery and one shot of Mesa Verde. "Does this spark your memory at all? We think this is where your ancestors came from. There used to be thousands of your people, and then suddenly they vanished. A few of them formed into other tribes, but no one knows why you built these easily defensible fortresses, and then why you left."

"You're wrong," Suski said.

Coya spoke. "But—"

"No, you're wrong," he said, and pulled the book away from me and stuffed it into his backpack.

"Why are you so angry all the time?" I asked.

"Wouldn't you be angry if you were living as a prisoner? I am in a nice building, but I know my people are living in the cold. I look out the windows and see this snow and I know that they are suffering, and yet your people still hate my people."

"To be fair," I said, "your ship killed thousands of humans."

"That was an accident," he said, his white cheeks flushing just slightly. "We didn't have control over it." He seemed genuinely sorry.

"I believe you," I said.

"Most humans don't," he said, "or they wouldn't be treating us like this."

It was my turn for a deep breath. "Humans don't treat each other very well. It's not something we're good at. And we're afraid when someone looks different from us."

"You look different from the other students," he said. "Your skin is brown, and your hair is black and blue."

"And you have no idea the kind of crap humans give each other about skin color," I said. "You'd think it wouldn't matter, but it does."

"I don't understand 'crap,'" he said, and I laughed. I couldn't help it.

"I'm not going to translate that one," I said. "What I mean is that humans don't treat humans very well. It's been that way for a long time. Maybe that's something that your father can teach us?"

"Maybe it is," he said.

"I hope so."

THIRTEEN

Kurt met me at the door to the Ghouls dorm with two dozen pink roses in a handmade glass vase. He was grinning from ear to ear.

"How did you get these?" I said, excited and smelling them. "Wait—don't tell me. It's more fun to imagine how you snuck past the guards."

"It was really—"

"Hush!"

"I almost died getting them for you."

"That's more like it!"

"Well, I have a busy schedule planned out for us."

"I should hope so," I said, and took his hand.

Kurt led me to a conference room in the old part of the school, where he had put two place settings on a table along with covered plates from the cafeteria.

He tried to pull out my chair as if we were in a fancy restaurant, but that never works very well, so I just thanked him and adjusted it on my own.

Kurt had chosen fettucine Alfredo from the cafeteria: carbs, butter, and cheese. Apparently he and I were kindred spirits. Not in an *Anne of Green Gables* kind of kindred spirit way, but a cute kindred spirit who smelled nice and made a good snuggling companion on the couch. A Gilbert Blythe kindred spirit, not a Diana Barry.

We ate and talked, and when we were done, he revealed two more dishes under plate covers: cherry cheesecake. I've never been much of a cherry kid, but this one was very, very good.

And as we ate, I spilled the news about the Guides. He listened closely and asked all the right questions at all the right places, and he held his plate wrong and a cherry rolled off it and it landed on his jeans, which meant that he was paying attention at the expense of his dignity, which was what I needed.

After dessert, Kurt led me up to the third floor, to a wing I'd never been in before. We stopped in front of a locked door, and he pulled out a key with a big tag on it that read "Museum."

"So this is the famous museum?"

"A small one."

"Why didn't you take me here before? And how did you get the key?"

"I hardly knew you. You don't take just anybody to the museum. Well, actually, this was the first time I was able to talk the assistant principal into giving me the key. Having the school guarded by the FBI had a lot to do with that. The G-men are guarding every door. It'd be a lot harder to sneak out the *Mona Lisa* with them watching."

He turned the lights on. Apparently Kurt has a spy on the inside of my soul and knew exactly where I'd like to go without me even knowing such a place existed. The museum had three Rembrandts! It also had a Rothko, and I stared in amazement at the giant slabs of color, the grays and blues and bright oranges and yellows. There was something about standing in front of such beautiful artwork that gnawed at me, reminding me of what I'd said to Suski about humans hating humans. People who hated shouldn't be capable of creating something so perfect, so vibrant and full of life—full of life even though the creator had been dead for a hundred years.

All of the paintings, etchings, and woodcuts were enclosed in glass, and I could practically feel the electricity humming through the room's security system. And the electricity flowing through me.

It was somewhere between the portrait of *Dr. Paul Gachet* and *The Olive Trees* series that I reached over and took Kurt's hand. It was warm and soft.

"I've always wanted to paint," he said.

"Why don't you?"

"Laziness, I guess," he answered with a grin. "I've taken art classes and I'm always frustrated by how not good I am. I know the solution is to practice practice practice, but I don't have the patience. Or the drive. It's like I want to know how to paint, but I don't want to learn how to paint." He paused. "That probably makes me sound like a loser."

"I'm the same way with languages," I said. "I'd love to know a second language. A lot of people speak Spanish in Miami, and people always think I'm Cuban or Puerto Rican because of my coloring, so they'll speak to me in Spanish. I learned a few words. I can count to twenty and I can order at a restaurant, but I've never forced myself to study."

"How's this for lazy," he said. "I'm technically Indian—that's where my citizenship is—born in Hyderabad. But I only speak English. I could get deported one of these days and have to go back home and work in a call center or something."

"Would they really deport you?"

"I've applied for citizenship," he said. "But there's a long waiting list. I wonder what they'll do about the Guides' citizenship. They landed in America—does that make them American? It's not like we can load them on a bus and send them back to where they came from. Besides, from what you said, putting them on a bus would just be shipping them back to Mesa Verde, right?"

"I don't see us creating a new little nation for them," I said. "We've seen how well that's worked out in the past, with Native American reservations."

"So they'll be part of the melting pot?" Kurt asked.

"I don't know what they'll be," I said. "These Guides are going to need a lot of education, and they don't have any money. Are we just going to give them free houses?"

"That's probably what Mai is discussing with the president," Kurt said. "Maybe they'll trade the spaceship for land. I bet that's it. Wasn't your dad talking about what an amazing treasure trove the ship is?"

We moved in front of the portrait of *The Suicide of Lucretia* by Rembrandt, on loan from the Minneapolis Institute of the Arts. She was holding a knife, having stabbed herself rather than being forced to sleep with a tyrant king. The beautiful image showed an angelic, sorrowful girl, blood creeping down her dress.

I nodded. "Look at this girl," I said, staring into the weeping eyes of *The Suicide of Lucretia.* "Imagine having to make a sacrifice like that—to have to kill yourself in order to stand up for your principles. Well, she was killing herself for love, I guess."

"Would you do that?" he asked. "Kill yourself for love?"

I smiled at him and squeezed his hand. "It's all very romantic, but I'd rather not kill myself for anything."

"Sure," he said. "But would you do it?"

"How do you even answer that?" I said with a little laugh. "Yes, I'd love to be that in love with someone where I feel that passionately. But it's a little hard to imagine. What about you?"

"I don't think I've ever been in love before," he said. "Not really. Heck, I can't even honestly say that I'd kill myself for my parents. That probably sounds awful, but I feel like I know you and Malcolm and Brynne and Joshua better than I know them."

"That's got to be rotten."

We moved to the next painting.

"I just don't really have a strong connection with anyone, not enough to stab myself over."

The next painting was a massive oil—*The Death of Germanicus.* It showed a Roman general dying in bed, surrounded by fawning and weeping loved ones and dedicated soldiers.

"Now this," Kurt said, "is how I'd prefer to die."

I read the card next to it. "It says he was poisoned."

"Okay. This is not how I'd prefer to die," he declared. "But it's how I'd like my deathbed to be. Not all alone holding a knife and bleeding. Surrounded by all my adoring fans."

"I'd be there," I said.

"The woman crying?"

"No, the soldier holding a spear. I'd protect you."

"Too late. I've been poisoned."

★ ★ ★

The next stop on our date was the foosball table in the common room.

"Foosball?" I asked with a grin. "You're so romantic. And where is everybody? Every other time I've been in here, there's been a line of people waiting to play the winner."

"You mean Kenny Sonomura?"

"Yeah." No one had beaten Kenny in months, or so I'd heard.

"I paid him ten bucks to take all the balls and walk away tonight." Kurt dug into his pocket and produced four miniature soccer balls.

"Well, don't you just know how to show a girl a good time."

We played and played, and even though I was terrible, it was one of the most fun things I'd done since coming to this school. Kurt took it very seriously, making amazing, well-planned diagonal attacks and ricochets into the goal. I focused on defense, and when my goalie made a wild, random shot that bounced off four guys and two walls and scored—well, I did not acknowledge my point with quiet dignity.

He won 7 to 1.

And then he won 7 to 3, and then 7 to 4, and I pledged that I would learn the art of foos and return to crush him.

Finally, he said he had one more surprise for me, and he led me upstairs again to the third floor. He pointed me toward another hallway I'd never taken. It led up to a dark landing and a locked steel door.

He put the key in the lock and struggled to turn it.

"Where do you get all these keys?" I asked him, laughing a little loudly.

"I paid off the janitor," he said, and finally succeeded in turning the key. The door opened a few inches, and there was pale light and a breeze.

A huge grin spread across my face, and I helped him push the door open wide enough for us to slip through onto the roof of the Minnetonka School for the Gifted and Talented.

Kurt put his arms around me, wrapping me up in his warmth while we watched the occasional car drive past. Jack Frost was nipping the hell out of my nose, but I leaned in closer to Kurt and put my face into his neck. He felt warm and comfortable and just right.

Kurt pointed out constellations. Not in an *I'm the big educated man teaching my mindless girlfriend* sort of way, but in a nice *I've been up here before and you're going to love this* sort of way.

And did I say "girlfriend"? I don't know what you're talking about.

Just as I was craning my neck to kiss him, the entire world went to shit.

A siren sounded from somewhere, and Kurt confusedly said, "Tornado alarm?"

Then we heard the movement of well-greased military

vehicles as two trucks seemed to appear from nowhere—hidden by camouflage netting down on the grass—with missiles on their backs, rising and turning toward the east. Two soldiers ran out onto the roof, and one ran over to us, yelling for us to get inside, down to the basement.

We didn't have to be told twice. We ran as fast as our snowy shoes would let us on the stone floor. I was wearing rule-breaking heels, too, and had to hold on to Kurt's arm as we went.

"Surface-to-air missiles," he muttered. "What does Suski have to say about this?"

When we got to the common room, a huge group of students was filing through in the direction of the basement, but they'd all stopped to look at the TV. Kurt and I moved to the cafeteria, where there was a smaller group. Rachel saw me and waved.

The big TV was now showing a shot of the Minnesota Governor's Residence, shaky cam, and then we saw a slow-motion replay of something landing on the lawn. It was triangular and big—about the size of half a basketball court. Figures emerged from it. Guns were fired. There was an explosion. And then nothing. Just back to the shot of the Residence, a shiny black ship parked on its lawn.

"We don't know what's going on," the commentator stammered. "But there appears to have been an attack on the Governor's Residence. We can see armed personnel—possibly aliens?—advancing on the building from what appears to be another spaceship—yes, another spaceship. This one did not crash-land. Its inhabitants have forced their way into the Residence."

The cafeteria was in mayhem, but I ducked under arms and squeezed between people to get closer to the TV.

"I knew it was invasion," someone said as I passed them. "I told you it was invasion."

The news broadcast kept changing camera angles—from the view of the front lawn to a view of the back lawn, to a shot inside the empty press room. But nothing was happening anywhere. The reporter kept saying that soldiers—American soldiers this time—were advancing on the building, but I didn't see them. It was too dark, and the cameras were too far away. Smoke was rising from the front door.

Kurt appeared at my side and took my hand.

"What is this?" he murmured.

"I don't know," I said. "But it isn't good."

"Do you think Suski and Coya are in on it?"

I shook my head, but I didn't know. I didn't want to believe it. They weren't bad—they were misunderstood and they were hated, but they weren't bad. I strained to see them in the group, but couldn't spot them.

"This ship may have come from the crashed craft in Minnesota," the commentator speculated. "We're checking with air traffic control to see if they have a statement."

"It couldn't have come from there," I said, and was aware that tears were coming down my face. "My dad would have found it."

"And why the Residence?" Kurt asked.

I looked at him, my heart beating wildly. "Maybe they're not here for the president. Maybe they're here for Mai."

All of the adults: the FBI, the RAs, the chefs, the secretary, the grief counselor—they all tried to get us downstairs, but then the screen changed to a small press briefing room and the whole school went quiet.

The president stumbled into view, his clothes rumpled, like he'd been getting ready for bed. Mai was shoved in the room after him, still wearing the white mummy-bandage suit that we'd seen on all of the Guides. The governor was brought in last, mauled and obviously dead.

And then we saw it. Them. They were beasts—two feet taller than everyone else in the room, with gray scaly skin and faces full of thorns, some drawn back and pointing behind, and some protruding forward. They looked like enormous spiny lizards. Each one had four arms and a set of mammoth legs, and each hand had two fingers and a thumb. They were carrying devices I didn't recognize, but they had all the earmarks of guns.

The creatures wore the same earpieces the Guides wore, with the same speakers on their chests. But their mouths were covered with masks that looked almost like muzzles.

The sound of gunfire came from somewhere off camera, but the two monsters seemed unfazed. One of them stayed by the door while the other marched up to Mai and the president, both of whom were trying to act brave in spite of everything. The president even took a step in front of Mai, to get between him and the monster, but the monster batted him aside easily and grabbed Mai by the shoulder, his talonlike fingers gripping into the flesh of Mai's shoulder. Blood sprouted across the white suit, and Mai cried out.

The beast spoke, his voice harsh and acidic.

The translator spoke his words. "Is this where I talk to the humans? Are the humans watching?"

Someone off camera shakily said that yes, the cameras were rolling.

"We've been monitoring your communications," the translator said. "And we've come to correct an error in the facts."

He shoved Mai forward, and Mai let out a cry of pain.

"You've been told that this man is to be your Guide. That he has great wisdom to impart, in exchange for letting him live here on your world."

Kurt glanced at me. My tears had stopped.

"This man is no Guide," the monster said. "He is a leader, I'll grant you. But he is a leader of slaves. He is a leader of a people we grind under our feet. Who are less than the food we eat. He is a leader of drones. That is what your Guides are. Drones. Living shells who exist only to benefit us. He has lied to you. And he will pay for his lies."

And with that, the monster grabbed Mai's injured shoulder, lifted him from the floor, and rammed another clawed hand into Mai's chest.

"And so we will do to all of our property," he said. "To this man's children, and their loved ones."

He dropped Mai to the floor, who fell motionless out of the camera shot. All that remained now was the broken podium, the two monsters, and the president.

The beast pointed his gun at the camera, and everything went to static.

I looked at Kurt. "We've got to find Coya and Suski." He nodded, and we pushed our way back through the crowd of horrified people.

FOURTEEN

I yanked off my shoes and then ran down the hallway toward the Ghouls dorm. Other people were running, too; it felt like the whole school was in a state of panic. We'd seen the real aliens. They were the ones we had feared would come out of the crashed spaceship, and they were every bit as bad as we had suspected.

"Mutiny," I said to Kurt as we ran toward the girls' dorm. "That's what all the murder scenes were. It was mutiny."

As I threw the door open and turned down the dorm hallway, all the pieces seemed to come together in my mind.

"The rooms were too big—that was one thing we noticed—the ceilings were too tall, and we thought that was weird."

"And the room," Kurt said. "The murder room. You said that those beds were bigger than the rest."

"Yes! There were these awful aliens on board, and they were keeping the Guides as slaves, and the slaves mutinied."

My phone buzzed, and I pulled it from my pocket.

"Dad," I said. "Are you okay?"

"We're mobilizing for World War Three down here," he said.

"Dad, be careful."

"Don't tell me to be careful," he said, his voice more stern than usual. "You be careful. I know you. The alien specifically mentioned Mai's children."

"I know, Dad," I said. "I'll be careful."

"I want you to get out of here. Out of state. I want you to go to Grandma's. Not Grandma Goodwin, but Grandma Tanner."

"New Mexico is, like, a thousand miles from here," I said.

"More than a thousand miles," he said. "And that's where I want you. Off the grid. Out of touch. It'll be the safest place."

"Dad, I can't leave my friends."

"Then take them with you," he said. "But get out. That'll be the last place anyone will be fighting."

"What about you?" I was holding back tears.

"I'll be fine," he said. "I'm with the army. Someone has to save the world, right?"

I smiled through my tears. "Dad, it was mutiny, wasn't it?"

"That's my guess, too," he said. "Now hang up, and drive.

I don't imagine cops will be handing out a lot of speeding tickets, and Bluebell is fast."

"I love you, Dad."

"Love you, too."

Nobody cared as Kurt ran down the hall of the girls' dorm and we threw open the door. Rachel reached the door about the same time I did, coming from the other direction. She was a sobbing mess, while Brynne looked like she was ready to find a machine gun and take the aliens on single-handedly.

"Where's Coya?" I asked, out of breath.

"The FBI came for her," Brynne said.

"Where are they taking her?" Kurt asked.

"They said they were taking her—Suski, too—to the bunker."

"I know where that is," Rachel said. "I think they're talking about the old tornado shelter. I used to go there to get some peace and quiet. Until I saw a rat."

"Let's get down there," I said.

"Why?" Kurt asked. "Won't the FBI be able to protect them?"

I paused for a minute. It was true. Plus there were camouflaged surface-to-air missiles out on the property. Did they really need us?

"Rachel," I said. "Lead us to the top of those stairs. I want to go down there if we have to."

She nodded. We grabbed a few things that we thought we

might need—sweaters, keys, Rachel's pepper spray, Brynne's brass knuckles, which, I think, were illegal to even own. She just smiled and said that she'd only had to use them once, on a blind date who was all hands.

We ran to the old part of the school, following Rachel to the basement. Just as we rounded the corner, we came face-to-face with two FBI agents, guns drawn.

"Where are you going?" one demanded.

"Trying to get to a safe place," I said.

"We're advising all students to—"

He stopped as we heard the explosive whoosh of rockets being fired.

"They're here," I said. "How many agents do you have?"

"Four," he said. "We're going to keep you safe. Just head down that hallway and cover in place. Sit with your back against the wall, put your head between your knees. Wait for instructions."

"It's okay," I said, talking as quickly as I could think, which is never good. "We're leaving."

"That's your choice," he said.

"We're taking Coya and Suski with us," I said.

He half smiled, but his face was dead serious. "No, they're under lockdown."

"No," I argued. "They said they're coming after the children of Mai. That's Coya and Suski. They've already fired rockets. Those aliens—those things—are here."

There was the chatter of machine-gun fire outside.

"They'll be safer here where we can keep an eye on them," he said. "This isn't your decision to make."

"No," I said. "It's your decision. But think about it: just a handful of those things got through the Governor's Residence security. Do you have anywhere near their manpower? We're going to be the next target, because we're not protected. Half the U.S. army is down at the spaceship, at the camps where the Guides are. But aliens—these bad, psycho aliens—are coming here."

He looked back at the other agent in the foyer.

"Where will you take them?"

"If I tell you, they could torture it out of you," I said.

He thought for a minute and then shook his head. "No. No way. I'm not turning over our responsibility to a couple of teenagers." There was a boom, loud and close. It shook dust from the plaster ceilings and the fire alarm went off. Every twenty feet a light high on the wall flashed bright and fast, and a siren blared.

"I can see the parking lot door and it's fine. I watched Hannah and Emily both get in their cars and get away from here," I yelled to the agent, and he had responded, which meant the new aliens had come in through a different door. If they'd come in through his, he'd be dead.

"The explosion could have been one of our RPGs," he said, although he plainly didn't believe it.

A moment later the fire sprinklers turned on, heavy and soaking.

"Give them to me before the aliens get down here," I pleaded. I needed to see Coya again. We'd grown closer than I had realized. Even stoic, grumbling Suski had grown on me.

The sound of gunfire was getting closer. "That's the National Guard," the agent murmured to himself. "Where are . . . East One, this is West One. Come in."

I couldn't hear a response—his radio was one of those little spiral cords that went up to his ear—but he made the call again. "East One, this is West One. Come in. East Two, this is West One. Come in."

There were two explosions in quick succession—giant, wall-shaking explosions, and I could only guess that those missile trucks had just been destroyed.

"Dammit," he said, turning back to me. "Your car fast? You a good driver?"

"Yes to both," I said. I almost hugged him. "We'll take care of them."

"Hurry," he said, and I followed him into the old part of the building, down a set of stairs, and then through a locked steel door.

The basement looked like an old musty library, with rows and rows of shelves. Coya and Suski were sitting on a pair of folding chairs. Coya jumped up and gave me a hug when she saw me.

"I am so sorry," I said. "I'm so sorry about your father."

"I'm sorry about our lies," Coya said.

"I don't care about that. We're going to get you out of here. To somewhere safe."

Suski looked up at the FBI agents, and the agent-in-charge nodded. "We can't protect this place. Not against that kind of firepower."

"Where are we going?" Suski said, standing up.

"You're coming with me," I said. "And we're leaving now. No time to pack anything."

The agent-in-charge turned to me and handed me his FBI badge. "If you get questioned by anyone along the way—if you run into roadblocks or get pulled over—show them this and have them call me."

"Thank you," I said, tucking the ID into my coat pocket. "We won't let you down."

"If there's a country left at the end of this, and if I still have my job, I want to hear from you."

"We'll be in touch. I'll keep them safe."

He turned to one of the agents. "Give me your Taser." The other agent very reluctantly pulled it from his holster.

"As long as I'm getting fired," the agent-in-charge said, "you might as well take this." He placed the gunlike device in my hand, and I took a deep breath.

He quickly showed me how to operate it—twenty seconds' worth of instruction, but enough to give me the gist. I could figure out the rest.

The six of us ran back out the door and up the stairs. Suski was still wearing his uniform, but Coya was dressed casually—a T-shirt and jeans that I recognized from Brynne's closet. Neither of them had coats. We'd have to stop somewhere and buy them. If any stores were still going to be operating now that the world was at war with aliens.

I wondered if the president was still alive.

I put Suski in the front seat—he was too broad-shouldered to fit in the back with the others. Coya was the smallest of us, and I asked Rachel if she could take the first shift holding her. Rachel nodded enthusiastically. "I can't believe we're running."

There were flames just off the road, and, like I'd guessed, the two trucks were burning. There was an armored vehicle by the front door, its back hatch open and empty. I couldn't see any alien ship, but there was a fire raging in the small commercial district just west of our campus. Had we knocked a ship out of the sky? It made me want to chant *USA! USA!* but the aliens were still in the school—the gunfire and the explosions proved that. The aliens were going to kill those FBI agents. Would they kill the students? Torture them for information? "Anyone want to bail, say so now," I said. "This is going to be dangerous. We have two people that some awful-looking aliens view as targets."

"That's why I'm coming," Rachel said, steel-faced. "We have to do something."

Brynne laughed, unease in her voice. "I'm just hoping that, at some point, I get to sit on Suski's lap." When I looked at her in the rearview mirror, I saw she was reaching across Kurt to hold Coya's hand.

"You're sure?" I asked them again.

"Yes," they both said, and Rachel added, "Just go already."

"I'm not letting you go without me," Kurt said.

Bluebell had been detailed and waxed by the transportation company and had a little bit of that new car smell that she had never lost and that awe-inspiring sheen that only a BMW 550i Gran Turismo can radiate. Zero to sixty in 5.2 seconds. 445 horsepower. Eight-speed automatic transmission. *Car and Driver* magazine called it "the fastest living room you'll ever drive." I think that was meant to be an insult, but this was a party car, designed to cram in all your friends and give them each their own TV. I personally have never stood up and reached to heaven through the sunroof, but I can't say that no one ever has. (It's easier to do that from the backseat.)

So, four people in the back was tight, but not as bad as you'd think.

"It was a mutiny, right?" I asked. We didn't take the

freeway—that would lead us past the crash site, and I knew that was a bad idea. I pulled up my GPS and found a route to Sioux Falls that took us southwest through Mankato.

"Yes," Suski said. "It was a mutiny. We are sorry we lied about it. We didn't see a choice."

"You were slaves?"

"Our people have been slaves on that ship for as far back as we can remember. A hundred generations, maybe. We do not know."

A light dawned in my head. "That's what those metal rings on the walls were for, weren't they? They were to lock you up."

"Yes," he said. "We were always chained."

Rachel spoke up. "So how did you mutiny?"

"We overwhelmed them. There were too many of us; they couldn't stop us, not even with their strength and weapons. But many of our people died."

"Why did you crash?"

"We didn't know how to pilot the ship," Coya said. "As you found out, we don't know how to read the language of our masters. We couldn't use their equipment. Our best people found this planet and tried to land. But they were guessing."

"And then," Kurt said, "you made up the story about being Guides? Why?"

Suski answered, anger in his voice. "We didn't want to

be slaves again. We wanted freedom. Now we will all be slaves—us and you. The Masters will not leave us alone. Now that they found us here, they will come in force."

The thought made me shudder. I pictured the alien killing Mai on TV. "How many more Masters are there?"

"We do not know," Suski said. "But they are strong and we are weak. And they are smart and we are not. They created that spaceship, and the one that attacked the school."

"Our planet can fight back," Brynne said. "Just like your people did."

"Many will die," Coya said.

"It doesn't matter," I said. "The Masters can't get away with this. We won't let them."

"It's worse than you think," Suski said. "They won't just go away. They need us. We were slaves on the ship, but we were more than slaves."

I heard Coya take a quick gasp. Disgust.

"What?" I asked, looking in the rearview mirror at her.

"I can't talk about it," she said, and looked out the window.

"We are how they breed," Suski said. "You said that you found tools—spikes and hooks. They are for stabbing. For surgery."

I heard Coya begin to cry, and I felt my stomach start to turn.

"The spike is used to insert a parasite in our abdomens, men and women. It grows in us, in our bellies. When it gets too big, it . . . I don't want to say."

"Say!" Brynne and Rachel said together.

"The parasites begin to eat their way out," he said. "They are monsters, vermin. Even the Masters can't control them. They are removed from the body with spikes and hooks, chained and grown in cages until they become like our Masters. Those who go through it do not survive."

"That's horrifying," Rachel said.

"We had to make the decision," Suski continued, "when we mutinied, that all those who had been implanted had to be killed. They were all willing. We offered them a merciful death, rather than a death of pain and terror."

Coya continued for him, her voice shaking with tears. "That was what our ship was for. It was a breeding ship. All of us knew that eventually we would be forced to die."

"Wait," I said. "A thousand Guides committed suicide in the ship. Is this why?"

Rachel gasped.

Coya spoke, her voice small and tremulous. "Yes."

"I'm so sorry," Brynne said.

"No," Suski said. "They were proud to die. They killed themselves to give the rest of us freedom."

There was silence in the car for a long time, as we tried to get through the chaos of the streets without making us look like a target. I followed the speed limit, stuck to side streets, made a reasoned course toward the freeway.

"What about Mai?" I asked. "He was very old. I thought no one got old."

"There were some who were instructed to control the rest of us. To be in charge of us. Coya and I would have served that role. We would not have been killed. But now, the Masters want us more than any others," Suski said. "You asked why we have no mothers. It is because we choose not to get attached to our children in the same way you do. We don't speak of mothers. When you ask us about mothers, we do not reply. We do not get attached to one another the same way you do."

Coya nodded. "Long ago we decided that we would not breed, not our people. We thought that if there were not enough of us—if we never had children—the Masters could not survive. They forced breeding—artificially."

"And the children are raised by slaves who are not their mothers. A mother would love her baby too much and smother it—that was the way of it," Suski said. "Everyone on that ship wanted to die early because they expected to die horribly."

"Suski and I are brother and sister," Coya said. "We know that Mai is our father. Most of our people do not know who their fathers are. And no one knows who their mother is. If the Masters are ever gone, it would be our duty to go to our people and lead them."

There was silence in the car for a long time. I couldn't believe what I had just heard. I knew the world was terrible, but it wasn't terrible like this. And these people had landed on Earth expecting a better life and instead were met by angry protests and forced to live in tent cities. If there was anyone who deserved a good life, it was the Guides.

"Just one more question," I said. "Why no shoes?"

Coya laughed, a wet, crying laugh. "That was just something Suski and I decided. Because we'd never walked in shoes before, and it looked hard."

"It is hard," Suski said.

I laughed, and then Brynne and Rachel laughed, and then Kurt did, and soon we were all laughing, and Suski was pulling his shoes off, exposing his bare feet.

FIFTEEN

It was twenty minutes before midnight when we rolled through Sioux Falls. A light rain was falling, just enough to keep the wipers on their lowest setting.

We pulled over to get gas, and Suski slumped low in his seat. The rest of us got out to stretch our legs. With her makeup on, Coya was indistinguishable from any other pale-faced girl.

Brynne was glued to her phone, finally in a place where we got good reception, and Rachel went into the store to stock up on snacks.

"Are you all right?" I asked Suski, when it was just him and me in the car.

He looked out the windows thoughtfully. "I worry about my people. We may be safe, but what about them?"

"They have the entire army guarding them," I said. "I mean, are *you* okay? Your father just died."

"I have to be strong," he said. "For Coya. For all of us."

"Hey, Suski," I said. "We're in this together. I don't know if you noticed, but there are six of us on this road trip. Not just you and Coya. We're all taking care of each other. I'm here to take care of you."

"You are kind," he said. "Humans are not always kind. And, in truth, you are not always kind."

"Listen," I said. "This isn't a pity party. This is an adventure. We're going on a road trip. You don't know what a road trip is, but it means fun."

"This is not supposed to be fun," he said. "This is supposed to be an escape."

"Did you know that sometimes humans use the word *escape* to mean fun? You probably don't know the word *vacation*—of course you don't—but this is what a vacation is. It's a bunch of people getting together and going somewhere. You talk and you eat and you listen to the radio too loud and you have fun. Yes, we're being hunted by horrible parasitic spiky monsters, but no vacation is perfect. It's better than being stuck in the middle seat on an airplane."

"I don't understand."

"It was a joke."

"You joke a lot."

"You don't joke enough," I said.

Kurt opened the door and got in. "Good news. I got everyone a Sioux Falls 'The Heart of America' shot glass. I would have gotten the fridge magnets, but then one of us would put our magnet on the car and Alice would freak out."

"Damn straight," I said.

I saw that Kurt was also holding a Lincoln High School Patriots sweatshirt and a Patriots stocking cap, and he handed both of them to Suski, who changed out of his blazer. I put the blazer in the trunk.

Brynne climbed in and then Rachel. Coya got assigned to sitting on Kurt's lap, and I gave him the look of death just before she sat down. He gave me a very innocent *Hot alien girls sit on my lap all the time* look.

"Okay," Brynne said. "I've been texting with Emily Fenton, and she says people died. She doesn't know who, but she saw bodies on the floor as she was running to evacuate. The aliens—the Masters—killed all the FBI, and she said she only saw one National Guardsman who was helping students evacuate. There was a fire in the building, but she doesn't know how bad."

"What?" Kurt asked. "How many students? Who?"

"She has to be exaggerating," Rachel said. "That can't be right." Then, with a softer voice, she spoke to Brynne. "Did she give any names?"

"Only a few." Brynne paused. "Benjamin Widmer. Sara Glassman. Chani Armitage. Emily Renault. She says there were more. And Hannah's car got hit as she was trying to drive away, but she got out and ran. She's okay."

We all let that sink in. Was it my fault? Was it because I'd rescued Suski and Coya? Did the Masters kill those others just because they were in the way? Collateral damage? Or were they killing people to get information out of them—to find out where Suski and Coya went? To find out where I had taken them? This *was* my fault.

Rachel looked up, her voice shaky. "I've been trolling the news online. The crash site got strafed several times, but they have no idea yet about casualties. Witnesses are saying anywhere from three to five small ships attacked, and they're estimating each ship has four to six Masters on it."

"What about the president?" Kurt asked.

"He's in the hospital," Brynne said. "They're not saying how bad he is. The vice president is in charge. At least fourteen Secret Service agents are dead. There's video of the aliens leaving in their ship from the Governor's Residence—someone fired a rocket launcher or something at it. Maybe a rocket-propelled grenade. It didn't seem to make a dent in the ship. But the missiles at Minnetonka took down two ships."

"Awesome," Kurt said, with a kind of dejected happiness.

"So the Masters are out there somewhere, either looking for us or planning to attack the tent city?" I said.

"Yeah," Brynne said. "But even if they found our room at

school, they wouldn't have any way of finding your grandma, right?"

"Right," I said. "I haven't even been there in three years. We send letters once in a while, but none since I've been in Minnesota. Plus, it's a PO box, so they couldn't find her house from it."

"My update," Rachel said, "is that I have a shopping bag full of pop and Oreos."

"Oh no," I said. "We do not eat inside Bluebell."

"Dude," Rachel said. "Oreos."

"Dude," I said. "Hand-sewn leather."

"I promise to eat very carefully."

"Ugh," I said. "I trust you, but it's Suski here I don't trust. He can't eat an Oreo cleanly to save his life."

He looked confused.

"Let me teach you," I said. "Rachel?"

I heard the bag tear, and I turned back to grab one.

"You put the whole thing in your mouth," I said, very seriously. "No half-bites. No unscrewing the cap and licking out the filling. No opening your mouth if the bite is too big. You keep your mouth closed and chew."

"I don't even want one," he said.

"That is blasphemy, and I won't have that in my car. We are on a road trip, and you will eat an Oreo. Rachel?"

She handed me another, and I put it in Suski's hand.

"Now," I said, "do you want to be cool or not?"

He looked uncertain.

Brynne piped up. "You want to be cool."

"I want to be cool."

"I want to be cool, too," Coya said.

"Rachel," I said. Another cookie was distributed.

"On the count of three, we all cleanly eat our Oreo. Cleanly. One, two, three."

I shoved the whole Oreo in my mouth and waited until my lips were sealed around it before biting down. Suski let a few crumbs leak out from his lips, and he chewed awkwardly, then swallowed and opened his mouth to show me.

"Not necessary," I said. "Rachel, I trust you have Mountain Dew to wash down these Oreos?"

"I do indeed."

"Please distribute to my alien friends. And honestly, people, the Masters will be the least of your problems if you spill in Bluebell."

I put the car in gear and pulled out of the gas station.

"Does someone have something good to listen to on their phone?" I asked.

Everyone read through their top playlists. Rachel's was entirely too much classical music—she really loved the cello—and Brynne was a Top 40 girl. Kurt's was an adequate mix of popular stuff and indie rock, so he won. I plugged it into Bluebell, and we headed west into South Dakota.

South Dakota was flat and straight, and my GPS told me

the road went for 130 miles through farmland without turning. With all the confidence of German engineering and an FBI agent's ID badge, I laid the pedal down and flew. We made thirty miles in just over twenty minutes.

"Crap," Rachel said. "Crap crap crap."

"What?" I asked, looking at her in the rearview mirror.

"Masters just hit that gas station in Sioux Falls," she said, the glow of her phone lighting up her face. "They just destroyed it. Massive explosion. Two ships."

"They tracked us there?" Kurt said. "Using our cell phone signals?"

"They must have," Rachel said, plainly starting to panic. "But why did they hit that and not out here?"

"My phone isn't getting any bars," Brynne said.

Kurt shook his head. "Neither's mine."

"Mine still has a few bars, but my GPS isn't working very well out here," I said. "It keeps blinking out."

I turned down the music and called my dad.

He answered on the first ring.

"You shouldn't call me," he said urgently. "Was that you in Sioux Falls? The security camera footage is already on the news. You have Suski and Coya with you, and the Masters are after you."

"Yeah, they're following us."

"Two ships. Turn off your cell phones. Bluebell's got GPS, doesn't it? See if you can find the fuse that disables it."

"Okay," I said, suddenly panicked. They couldn't be following us. That was the whole point of escape. I pulled over onto the shoulder and turned around to my friends.

"Guys, turn off your phones. Now."

"Aly," Dad said, using his *I'm trying hard to be a good dad* voice. "Why did you take them with you? I told you to get out."

"You told me I could take my friends with me."

"I thought you meant Brynne and Rachel."

"I know you did," I said. "I'm sorry."

I climbed out of the car and knelt down on the pavement, looking under the steering column for the fuse box.

"You need to hang up now," he said. "But, Aly, I love you. Be safe."

"I will. How will I call you?"

"Don't call me," he said. "Stay with Grandma Tanner until I come to get you."

"Okay," I said, pulling out the little fuse tweezers and searching for the right one. "Love you, Dad."

"Love you."

He hung up, and I suddenly felt very alone.

"Brynne," I said. "You've got an iPad. Is there any way to disable that? Airplane mode or something? Or, I don't know, just turn it off. Everyone else, turn off your phones and leave them off. Take out the batteries if you can."

"What happened?" Suski asked. We'd probably been

talking too much, back and forth and over each other, for his translator to keep up.

"A witness saw two of the ships heading west out of Sioux Falls," I said.

"Is there a place we can hide?" Suski asked.

"I don't know. And I don't know how long ago it was. Long enough that it's already in the news."

I found the fuse for the dashboard display and hoped it also controlled the GPS system. At the very least it would control the GPS interface.

"What if they looked at the video cameras from the gas station?" Brynne asked. "Is this because I was texting with Emily?"

"I don't know how it happened," I said, trying to stay calm.

"So what do we do now?" Kurt asked.

"I don't know," I said, suddenly angry. Why was everyone looking to me? Just because I had the car didn't make me in charge. And the fact that my dad worked for NASA didn't mean anything anymore—I didn't have my dad now. I've always had my dad.

Rachel opened her door and stepped out in the cool night air. She stretched and then reached down to help me up. "Let me take over for you," she said.

I nodded tiredly and hugged her. She was surprised, but hugged me back. I didn't let go, and soon I was fighting back tears. Everyone got out of the car then and stood around us. None of us knew what we should be doing, and I think we all felt stung. I regretted ever leaving Minnesota. We should have just gone to the crash site. I'd expected the Masters' spaceship to attack the tent city—which they did. That made sense. But why were they chasing us?

I turned to Suski and Coya.

"When you guys started at the school, we were told to treat you like royalty. That's why they're following us, right?"

"But we told you," Coya said. "It doesn't matter now. Not on the ship."

I sniffled and wiped my eyes again. "The Masters didn't get the memo."

SIXTEEN

The lack of motion woke me up. Rachel had pulled over on the side of the road—an interstate—and the sun was high in the sky.

I looked around and saw a motorcycle cop behind us with his lights flashing.

"Where are we?" I asked, face-to-face with Kurt, whose lap I was sitting on.

"Just outside of Colorado Springs," Rachel said. "Sorry."

"No worries. We have a Get Out of Jail Free card."

The cop came up to the window and looked inside. If he was startled by Suski's stark white skin, he didn't say anything.

"Do you know how fast you were going?"

"Around a hundred?" Rachel said. "But let me explain."

"Hang on," he said, and peered in the back windows.

"You've got too many people in the car, too. Can I see your license and registration?"

"My license is in the trunk," she said, and handed him the FBI badge. "But I'm supposed to show you this and have you call this number."

The cop looked at the badge, then back at Rachel. "Is this one of your friends? They answer the phone and pretend to be the FBI?"

"No," Rachel said.

I wished I was sitting in the driver's seat. I wanted to get out of the car, but I knew that always freaked out cops.

"Sir," Rachel said. "Can I get my license from the trunk?"

"I suppose you'd better," he said, and backed away from the car.

I couldn't hear them as they talked, and once she opened the trunk of the car, I couldn't even see them. The minutes seemed to drag on endlessly.

"How are you doing?" I asked Kurt.

"I remember that I used to have feet," he said. "But it's been a while since I've felt them."

I pretended to punch him in the stomach.

"Did I drool on you this time?"

"Not that I noticed."

The cop came back to the open driver's window and peered inside the car. "How are y'all doing?"

"It's my car, officer," I said. "If you want to talk to me."

"I want to talk to this young man," he said, pointing at Suski. "What's your name, son?"

Suski glanced back at me, and I nodded to him. *"Ho' Suski leshhina,"* he said, and then the translator said, "I am Suski."

"Well, I'll be," the cop said, and lifted his head out of the window. He stood there for a minute and then walked back to Rachel.

"Is this bad?" Suski asked.

"No," I said. "I think the cop will call that number."

"What is a cop?"

"Someone who keeps the peace," I said. "Like a guard. Someone who makes sure people follow the rules. Rachel broke a rule by driving too fast."

"She was driving very fast."

We waited for what seemed like a very long time.

"Have you slept, Suski?"

"I have not," he said. "I am enjoying the ride. I did not imagine a world could be so big—that you could go so far in one direction."

"You ain't seen nuthin' yet," Brynne said with a smile. "The world is a lot bigger than this."

"How about you, Coya?" I asked. "Have you slept?"

"Yes," she said. "Not well, though."

Rachel closed the trunk and came back into the driver's seat. "I think everything's going to be okay."

I could see the cop clearly, as he stood beside his motorcycle, the FBI badge and Rachel's license in his hand as he spoke into his radio. He was talking a lot, but it was probably a big deal that he'd seen an alien all the way out here.

Finally, the cop walked back and handed the badge and license to Rachel. "Good news," he said. "Your story checks out. Better news, I'm going to give you a police escort to the state line, and we've alerted all the cops along the way to clear the path."

"You did what?" I asked. "We're trying to stay incognito!"

"We just want to keep you safe, ma'am," he said.

"They traced us to Sioux Falls. Now they'll know the road we're on and the direction we're going."

"I'm going to be going along with you," he said. "You're going to be safe."

I couldn't believe it. We thought that we'd thrown them off our trail—thought that we'd disappeared, and now everyone with a police scanner knew where we were.

I opened the door. "Rachel, I'm driving."

"Please," she said, getting out of the car.

"I'm sorry if this isn't what you wanted," the cop said. "We're only trying to help."

"It's too late," I said, walking around to the driver's side of the car. "What's done is done. This had just better not make the news."

"I'll follow right behind," he said, obviously sorry, but I

was too upset to be nice. "Drive as fast as you safely can. I'll keep up."

"How far is it to the border?" I asked. The faster I could make it, the sooner we'd be off the radar again. Assuming the news didn't travel to New Mexico.

"About a hundred miles. I think we're at mile marker one-oh-five."

"Okay," I said, and plopped down in the front seat. The backseat shuffled again. "If you've got my back, I'm going to open her up and see what she'll do."

"I've got your back," the cop said. "Be safe."

Come on, 445 horses, don't fail me now. I wanted to show off Bluebell's zero-to-sixty power, but a momentary flash of compassion kicked in and I decided not to spray the cop with gravel.

I looked in the rearview for oncoming vehicles and, seeing none, pulled off the shoulder and onto the pavement. Then I punched it. The engine purred deliciously as it guzzled fuel and rocketed forward. In five seconds we were going sixty. In thirteen seconds we'd gone a quarter mile. There was a limiter on the car that topped out the speed at one fifty-five. I'd never hit that before, but I intended to try.

As I drove I kept my hands at ten and two, just like I'd been taught in driver's ed—no point getting sloppy now. But I kept having the urge to look through the sunroof, just to see if we were being followed by a spaceship.

They couldn't be scanning all communications everywhere, could they? They probably only found us the first time because they knew Brynne shared a room with Coya so they were targeting her phone. Or maybe they'd been targeting my car because they knew I shared a room with Coya, too. But none of that meant they were checking the police radios.

I had to keep telling myself that to stop from hyperventilating. There was nothing especially safe about Grandma's house. There was nothing at Grandma's house. The only safety came from being off the map. We had to get back off the map. Once we hit New Mexico, I'd slow to the speed limit. No more possible slipups.

I handed my phone and memory card back to Kurt. "Call my dad. Tell him where we are and ask him to get some air cover."

"Are you serious?" he asked, putting the phone back together. "I'm calling to order fighter planes?" He found the number and dialed. "Next time we go on a date, you're planning it."

I glanced over at Suski. He was gripping the door handle tightly. He looked almost normal in his sweatshirt and cap—like any other high school boy.

I focused on the road and listened to Kurt relay the message to my dad. In a minute he hung up.

"Why are you doing this?" Suski asked, his voice quiet even though the translator spoke at the same volume all the time.

"Driving fast? Because I'm trying to get the hell out of Colorado."

"No," he said. "Why are you helping us? You could have left it for the guards at the school to protect us. Or the military."

Good questions. Stupid questions. Or maybe good questions and stupid answers.

"Because I like you guys," I said, and it sounded lame. "From the day you first arrived, I've felt a kinship with you. Maybe it's because we're both different, or maybe it's because we're both new."

"I don't know 'kinship,'" he said.

"It means you feel like family. Maybe you don't know family either. It means you feel like my brother and sister."

What was I doing? *Focus on the road, Goodwin.*

"Brother and sister," he repeated.

"Yes," I said. "No."

"What do you mean by 'yes no'?"

"I mean that I'm driving," I said. "I need to concentrate on driving."

We crossed into New Mexico, and I immediately slowed the car down to what felt like a snail's pace. We were still on the interstate, and a Colorado state trooper waved at us as we passed him at the border.

There was no fast way to get to my grandma's house. That was one of the problems with living on the reservation—the roads were few and far between, and the roads that I was willing to take Bluebell on were even fewer. The fastest route would be to go south through Santa Fe, but the quicker we could get off main highways, the better. So we turned west after Raton and headed into the mountains. The thirty-five-mile-per-hour speed limit through twists and turns of forested roads seemed harder to maintain than the blistering pace we'd been traveling at for the last day.

I glanced over at Suski and laughed a little to myself.

"What?"

"You're a little green man," I said.

"I don't understand."

"That's what we always thought aliens would look like," I said. "Little green men."

"I still don't understand."

"That's okay," I said.

Brynne spoke up. "She means you look sick. Drink more Mountain Dew. It'll settle your stomach."

"Is that true?" Rachel asked.

"I don't know," Brynne said with a simple shrug. "I've heard that before—that carbonation settles your stomach."

"No one is allowed to puke in my car," I said. "And,

Brynne, aren't you supposed to be a doctor or something?"

"I'm seventeen," she said. "Don't trust me."

We stopped for gas again in a little resort town called Eagle Nest. It was amazing how much warmer it was here than in Minnesota. We were in the mountains, but it was easily in the fifties, if not pushing sixty. I decided that I was going to find a new boarding school somewhere in New Mexico.

After filling up, I went in the store and tried to snoop, wondering if anyone would recognize Bluebell from any descriptions on the news or police scanners. There was nothing in the flimsy local paper, but it didn't publish every day. I struck up a conversation with the woman behind the counter—just idle chat about the weather and the big lake that was across the valley. She seemed disinterested, which was what I wanted. Disinterest. Boredom. No panic or curiosity. As far as she could tell, we were just a bunch of regular teenagers on a regular road trip.

Finally, I asked her specifically if she'd heard anything about the aliens, and she said that someone else had come in and told her that four fighter jets from Kirtland Air Force Base had shot down an alien ship in Colorado just a couple hours ago. She didn't have more details than that, but that was enough for me. For now, at least.

I bought Suski a baseball cap for Philmont Scout Ranch and an Eagle Nest T-shirt. He switched it in the parking lot, and I tried not to lose all feeling in my extremities when I saw his abs as I stuffed the Sioux Falls gear into the trunk. I explained what the writing on his new clothes meant and then we got back into the car.

It was stupid. I knew that the Masters knew we'd been in Sioux Falls, so I wanted to hide anything that said Sioux Falls. They wouldn't be trying to identify Suski by the writing on his hat, but still, it was something I could do, and I wanted to do everything I could, no matter how small.

The next city we drove through was Taos, but the highway didn't take us near Taos Pueblo—probably the most famous pueblo in the world. It was gorgeous and had been photographed and painted and drawn by every artist who had passed through here for a hundred fifty years. I told Coya and Suski about it, though. "It's like your ship, kind of. It's a place where people have lived in the same buildings for a long time—I don't know how long, but I want to say it's something like a thousand years."

"I still have trouble understanding years," Coya said.

"You're somewhere between sixteen and eighteen years old," I said to her. "I'm guessing. So imagine a building that's been there for a thousand years—Rachel, how many lifetimes is that?"

"Fifty or sixty," she said, almost without thinking.

"We don't know how long we were on the ship," Suski said. "It may be longer than that. Or less. There are stories of a time we didn't live on the ship. My father told them to me. Times when my people were happy."

"You'll be happy again," I said.

"Not with the Masters here. No one will be happy again."

"What if there aren't many Masters here?" I asked. "What if it's only a couple of ships? What if they're scouts? We've been able to successfully fight them off—the National Guard killed two of the ships just at the school. And a few more have been successfully shot down, one at the White House, and another one at the tent city. So, scouting ships."

Suski pointed to the Boy Scout logo on his hat, which I'd just spent five minutes explaining to him.

"No," I said with a laugh. "Not like that. I mean, what if they were sent ahead to find out what happened to all of you."

"Then the others will follow."

"You don't know that," I said. "This has never happened before. You've never been off the ship."

"They need us," Coya said. "For breeding. They need bodies to host the parasite."

Kurt spoke up. "That doesn't seem to be their mission. They're out for revenge. That little ship they have can't abduct many humans—it's too small."

"Then others will follow," Suski said again. He seemed so certain of it. But he had lived a life of fear and slavery—of course he'd be certain of it. It would be impossible to believe a world where these monsters didn't control everything.

It made me wonder if he always knew they'd be followed. Maybe that was why he never smiled.

I refused to believe it. Maybe their reality was like that, but my reality was that the good guys won and the bad guys lost. Maybe the bad guys did some really horrible stuff first, but the good guys fixed it. Was I naive? Probably. Almost certainly. But I didn't care. The good guys were going to win this time.

Eff you, Masters.

New Mexico was the Land of Enchantment. What I loved about it was that the nickname didn't refer to enchanting beauty or enchanting charms. It referred to real enchantment, like magic. There were twenty-three Native American tribes in New Mexico, and I'd been to many of their dances and feast days—especially when I was little and my mom was still alive. And there was something otherworldly about the state, something that made you wonder if it wasn't like any other place on Earth—if it was connected to something deeper. The people here lived simpler lives—my dad's parents often called the reservation a Third World country because so many people didn't have electricity or running water. To me it was peaceful, quiet, and—dare I say—spiritual. My grandmother's reservation was like a little string attached to my heart that never untied, that never let me forget that part of my heritage lived off the land.

I have always felt totally at home in the barrenness of New Mexico, despite the fact that I lived my whole life in lush, green Florida. There's something about sitting outside in the shade of a juniper, watching a stinkbug waddle across dry desert sand, while the buffeting wind is blowing through the sage behind you and the salt grass in front of you, and the horizon stretches out into the distance to some far-off monuments of sandstone. It makes you feel human.

There was more to New Mexico than that, of course. There was the food, which, next to seafood, was my favorite food on Earth. Green chile and mutton stew—I know that sounds gross, but that's because you've never been sick in a hogan, a traditional Navajo house, and had your grandma cook you a pot of stew while you lay on a stack of blankets.

And, yes, it's *chile* with an *e*. I don't know why that bothers so many people, but it's how it's spelled. Look it up.

We made a final pit stop at a grocery store in Cuba, New Mexico, just before entering the reservation. It was dinnertime, and we were all hungry—even Suski. After picking up a week's worth of groceries—mostly as a payment to my grandma for the surprise visit—we bought some fried chicken and potatoes at the deli. We sat at the picnic table outside the store and ate, mostly in silence. We were all exhausted and sore from almost a full twenty-four-hour drive.

"What if they're tracing our credit cards?" Rachel asked, chewing slowly.

"I thought about that, too," Kurt said. "But then why wouldn't they have found us by now? Just follow the gas receipts and look for a BMW. It's not like that car blends in."

"Maybe they're waiting till dark," Brynne said. "I mean, they attacked the Governor's Residence during the night. Sioux Falls, too. Maybe they like to be in the dark."

"This is the last place we'll use the credit cards," I said. "And we've probably got another seventy miles to Grandma's house. We'll do our best to hide the car when we get there." I thought of the shade houses that Grandma used to build during the summer, with canopies made of juniper boughs. We could do something like that to hide Bluebell. She'd probably get scratched, but that was better than the alternative.

Which meant, of course, that I was terrified. If I was willing to scratch my baby with pine needles, I had to be going out of my freaking mind.

I looked across the table at Kurt, who looked back at me and smiled through a full mouth. There was the tiniest wink—an indication that he knew I was having a rough time and he wanted to comfort me. He couldn't hold my hand right now, but he could wink.

I winked back.

Rachel held a newspaper and read while the rest of us ate.

"There was another attack," she said, finishing chewing a potato and swallowing it.

She suddenly had all our attention, as though a car hit its

brakes and squealed to a stop.

"The Utah Data Center," she said. "They have video—I bet it's all over TV."

"What's the Utah Data Center?" Kurt asked, a half second before the rest of us asked it.

"National Security Agency," Rachel answered. "Remember when there was that big scandal about how the NSA was listening in on everyone's phone calls?"

Coya looked at me. "NSA is not NASA?"

"No. NASA deals with outer space. NSA deals with communication."

"So what happened?" Brynne asked.

"The Masters shot up the place," Rachel said, and then looked at Coya and Suski. "Three ships, small ones. They demanded records about you two. The place went into lockdown. One thing can be said in the NSA's favor: they have cameras everywhere. So, when they couldn't get what they wanted, they left, but they gave us a really good look at their ships. It's the same kind that hit the Governor's Residence and included the same aliens—they've identified four."

"Four ships?" Kurt said.

"They've got to be scouts," I said. "Or they're just here to get revenge. Those ships are too small to abduct more than a dozen people."

"A missile put a hole in one," Brynne said, reading over Rachel's shoulder. "It was bombing the tent city. It was also identified as one of the ships that hit the NSA."

"Well," Kurt said, "this store has security cameras, and it looks like the Masters are trying to read our mail. I vote we get out of here."

We all took a bathroom break and I warned them that it was the last time they'd have running water for . . . I didn't know. How long were we going to be hiding out here? Until my dad came to get us—that's what he had said.

Back in the car, I turned on the radio, scanning through AM radio stations until I found one that came in clearly. We listened as we drove out west onto the reservation, gleaning what news we could. There hadn't been any attacks on the tent city today, but the air force had the skies over Lakeville filled with aircraft. While we'd been driving away from Minnesota, antiair missiles had been driven to Minnesota, and they were being set up all around the site. No one had seen any sign of the Masters' spaceships since Utah.

None of that filled me with confidence. They had to be somewhere. They couldn't have just fallen off the edge of the world. I mean, yes, that was exactly what a spaceship could do, but why? Why make threats and then disappear?

"They're not as powerful as they want us to believe," Brynne said, suddenly outraged. She was sitting on Suski's lap in the front seat (and probably loving every minute of it). "Maybe that's the whole reason they're hiding—they're in little ships that can get shot down. Maybe they know they'll lose if they try to attack the crash site."

"They are very strong," Suski said.

Brynne spoke. "You've only seen them being very strong—you haven't seen their spaceships. Rachel, what is the deal with our spaceships? They say that parts of them are as thin as tinfoil?"

"Right," Rachel said. "The one space shuttle crashed just because a piece of foam hit the shielding. And the other blew up because an O-ring got too cold."

"So I'm saying: what if their spaceships aren't very strong?" Brynne said.

"But in the news," I said, "they said one of them got hit by some kind of rocket, and they just took off and flew away."

"But maybe they're damaged," Kurt said, getting excited now. "Remember: they started with six ships—that we know about—and it sounds like they're down to only one."

Coya held her hands up. "You're all forgetting. We know these monsters. They are very strong. If they find us, we will die. There are not enough of us."

The car was silent for a long moment. I tried to guess how many aliens we were actually talking about—we saw two for sure. But maybe they'd left another in the ship? A pilot? And there had been some fighting taking place off camera. So were there four of them? There really could be as many as they could cram into that ship, but betting on at least four seemed reasonable.

"Guys," I said, letting out a long breath. "I'm sorry I brought you this way. We should have gone to the crash site. We'd be safer there."

"No," Suski said. "You are a good leader."

"No," I said. "I asked for you to come with me because I thought it would be better, safer. I thought I could protect you better than the FBI could. It's not working out that way."

"I think you're a remarkable person, Alice Goodwin," he said. "I don't think many humans would do what you have done. I don't think many of my people would do what you have done."

"They would have done something better, that didn't get us caught."

"No," he said. "You have done a good thing."

I took a deep breath and then let out a long sigh. "I don't know what the good thing is anymore. I'm scared."

"You don't have to be scared."

I glanced at him and forced a smile. "You'll protect us?"

"Ever since I was a boy I was taught that I was going to be the leader. I didn't know what to do, because there was so much death and I knew I couldn't stop it. What good is a leader when all they can do is help people who will die anyway?"

I smiled now, a real, exhausted one. "I feel like that right now."

"We may die," Suski said. "I knew long ago that I may

die, and I understand death. But I also learned that I can be a leader who helps people be happy whether they live or die."

"I wish you'd give me some lessons in that right now."

"You are teaching me lessons in it every moment," he said. "You are a good leader. Because you love those you lead."

I felt a tear roll down my cheek. "And what if we get caught?"

"Then we are caught, and we will die. But we will have been happy first, and it will be a good death."

A good death. That wasn't what I had planned for. No death—that was what I wanted. I wanted to keep my friends safe. Coya and Suski hadn't mutinied just so they could be torn to shreds by the Masters here on Earth. And Brynne, Rachel, and Kurt—they didn't sign up for any of this. They shouldn't be in the line of fire. They didn't know what they were in for when they came on this trip, when they became friends with the Guides.

The sun was down over the horizon when we rolled into the dusty cutoff of my grandma's town. There wasn't much there—the chapter house, three houses, and a water tower. It wasn't even really a town—it was a collection of dirt roads. If you drove down any of the roads far enough, you'd eventually run into a house.

I turned at the fence post that I recognized as hers. There was a pattern of reflectors on the steel pole so you could identify it in the dark.

We drove over a cattle grate and onto a hardpacked dirt road. A mouse skittered across our path in the headlights and disappeared into the brush at the side. I felt a lump in my throat—was I getting my grandma involved in our deaths, too? If the aliens were waiting for dark before they attacked, then shouldn't we expect them now?

The road wound around half a dozen bends in the mesa, and we passed a few houses before finally reaching a broad clearing. I pulled into the center, my lights resting on Grandma's hogan. It was the traditional home of the Navajos—round, made of logs, with a log-and-mud roof. A stovepipe came out of the center, and I saw smoke puffing out of it. Warm yellow light shone through the cracks around the door.

"Let me go explain, guys," I said, and pulled off my seatbelt. In Navajo tradition it was good manners to wait in the car until the person came out of her house and invited you up, but it was my grandma, and I figured it would be okay to break with tradition just this once.

I opened the car door just as she did, her short, thin frame silhouetted against the firelight behind her.

"Ya'at'eeh," she called out.

"Grandma," I replied, and hurried across the dirt to where she was standing.

"Is that my Alice?" she asked with a gasp. *"Sh'atsóí."*

"Shimasani," I said.

"You're so big," she said, reaching her arms out to me.

"Come here, you beautiful girl."

I grabbed her in a bear hug. We were so alike, my grandma and me—same height, same hair color. I was even named after her.

"I'm in trouble, *Shimasani*," I said, starting to cry. "We came here because we didn't know where else to go."

"Come in, child," she said, her voice strong and heavily accented. Her hogan smelled of cedar smoke and tea, and she pulled me inside, setting me on the bed beside her. She hugged me close. "Tell me what's wrong."

"I told you what's wrong when we talked on the phone. I'm in the middle of it," I said, and through sobs I explained how I'd ended up as friends with Coya and Suski, how I'd promised to protect them, and how we were on the run. I explained the parts that she probably didn't hear without a television or radio: about the mutiny, about the horrible life they'd had on the ship, always expecting death. And I told her how I'd come here, foolishly, seeking some kind of asylum—a refuge from all the problems of the world.

"We'll take care of you, baby girl," she said, rocking me in her arms. "We'll take care of you, *nizhóní*." She held my hand loosely in hers—her skin weathered from a life of living off the land.

I sniffled. "There are six of us," I said. "Your hogan is so small."

She laughed. "You are too used to your big house. We

can all fit. Have you eaten?"

I nodded.

"Well, take me out to meet these friends of yours."

I stood on shaky legs and led her by the hand to Bluebell. My friends were waiting by the car.

"Come meet my grandma," I said.

They came forward, Rachel first—she hugged Grandma and thanked her—and then Brynne. Kurt shook her hand, and Grandma turned to me and whispered far too loud, "I like him."

Then it was Coya's turn, and she stepped up to Grandma.

"Ho' Coya leshhina," she said, and the translator said, "I am Coya."

"Shimasani," I said. "This is going to sound crazy. Coya and Suski are Anasazi."

Grandma cocked her head and grinned wide, showing a few missing teeth. "So that's the magic in the Minnesota."

SEVENTEEN

We were all in the hogan, the door closed to shut out the cold, and we sat in a circle against the walls of the small house. Coya and Suski were speaking to Grandma. They were explaining everything that we had figured out. Brynne spoke up when her genetics research was needed, and I filled in a few gaps.

I leaned against Kurt's shoulder as we listened to the conversation. Coya explained her name, holding out her hair just as she had done with me—that *Coya* meant "beautiful." *Suski* meant "great warrior." Grandma laughed at that.

"We could use a great warrior," she said.

"A huge alien abduction," Kurt whispered to me. "I wonder if they left a crop circle."

Something changed in the conversation between Grandma

and the Guides, and she stood up and came and sat by me. "Shoo, little *ginnis glizhee*," she said to Kurt and the girls, and they all moved across the hogan. "I have to go speak with the Elders."

I got to my feet. "Do you want me to go with you?"

"No," she said. "Sleep. I fear we have a long way ahead of us."

"Why?"

She looked at the Guides. "I do not know what to do. I'm worried for you. You've seen much danger, and you'll see much more."

Grandma took a red velvet shawl from the bed and wrapped it around her shoulders, and then she placed a wide-brimmed hat on her head. I followed her to the door.

"Be careful," she whispered to me.

"I'm always careful," I lied.

"You're like your mother. You take risks."

"Hopefully they're good risks," I said.

"I'll be back," she said, and hugged me. *"Hágoónee'."* I watched from the door as she walked down the low slope to an old rusty pickup truck. She backed onto the road, and a moment later she had disappeared around a bend.

I felt a hand on my back and knew without looking that it was Kurt.

"Didn't you say something about hiding your car?"

I sighed. "Yeah. We'd better do it." I closed the door

behind us, and we stepped out into the dark. I shivered. It might not be as cold here as it was in Minnesota, but I wasn't wearing a coat, and it was still October.

Kurt walked around the south side of the hogan and poked through a few shelves.

"So what's your big secret?" I asked. "We've figured out Coya and Suski are human—Anasazi. What is it that you're hiding?"

"I'm not Indian," he said. "I'm Irish."

"You hide it well," I said, and let my fingers drag across his back as I stepped around him toward a shed.

"Maybe I'm secretly from Miami," he said. "Or how about I'm interning at NASA?"

"If we make it out of here alive, I bet we'll all be interning at NASA. We're going to have a spaceship-based economy."

I peered into the darkness of the open shed, trying to see if there was anything in there.

"Do I detect a hint of hopefulness in your voice? You're assuming we're not going to die?"

"Not assuming anything," I said. "You know what assuming does."

"I do indeed," he said, and squeezed past me into the darkness. "Chicken."

"I'm not a chicken," I said. "I was afraid I'd step on a rake or something."

He looked back at me, but all I saw was moonlight

reflecting on his glasses. "You really think your grandma has a lot of rakes? To keep the sand off of the sand?"

"There are trees," I said.

"Not trees with leaves," he said. "Here we go. A tarp!"

"You win," I said.

And then he appeared out of the darkness and before I knew it was happening, he was kissing me. Full-on kissing me. For a moment I was too stunned to react, but instinct kicked in and I grabbed his shirt, pulling him closer. The kiss was hard and frantic, as though each of us suddenly couldn't breathe without the other. He stepped closer, and my back bumped into the door frame. I felt like we were going to knock the shed down, and I didn't care—he was pushing against me and I was pulling him toward me, desperately, our lips and bodies moving together.

The wood of the shed creaked, and I laughed, breaking the kiss for just a moment before sliding my fingers through his hair and pulling his mouth back to mine. He tasted like he smelled—that perfect autumn scent, now combined with wood smoke.

He pulled away just enough to talk, his lips flicking against mine as he spoke. "We could have been doing this in a more comfortable place than a shed. Remember that next time you want to fall asleep on a couch."

"I'm not the one who cut our date short," I said. "Blame the aliens." I kissed him again.

"Damn aliens," he said, and wrapped his arms around my shoulders, pulling me all the way to him, kissing my ear and my hair.

"You know," I said. "I don't normally do this. Kiss boys I've only known for a couple of weeks."

"You usually wait at least three, huh?"

"At least."

I kissed him again, slow and lingering. I didn't know when I was going to get to do it again. Finally, I let him go, and we split apart. I was breathing heavily and could feel my face flushed. I wasn't shivering anymore.

"Where's that tarp?" I asked.

He took a deep breath. "Oh yeah. The tarp."

I pulled Bluebell around the back of the hogan—not that that would matter to a spaceship, but it made me feel better to have it out of sight of the road—and we unrolled a canvas tarp over the car. I cringed with every roll, worried it was rubbing sand against the paint and scratching my baby. When it was done, I took Kurt by the hand and we walked back to the door of the house.

I wanted to kiss him again—and again and again—but if we kept at it we'd never stop, and there were other things going on that were more important. I opened the door and went inside.

It was warmer now, the flame in the stove glowing brighter than it had been. We sat down in the circle around the stove. Rachel held up a box of crackers and another box of cookies. I reached for the cookies.

"So," Brynne said, looking at Coya. "Does this make sense to either of you? The whole 'you used to live out here and got abducted' thing?"

Suski shook his head, but Coya nodded slightly and spoke. "Tell them about the return voyage."

"We don't know if that's true," he said.

"Then tell them what we know," she said, and then, "I'll tell them. The thing is, we don't know how the ship was piloted. We don't know who steered it toward this planet, because, like you've seen, none of us can read. Even our father couldn't read. But someone directed the ship. And when we mutinied, we asked our father where we were going, and he simply told us we were going home. He told us that many times—it was a very long voyage."

I thought of the mess in the ship, of the blood that had never been cleaned up. "It was a long voyage?"

"It was a difficult voyage," Suski said. "We did not know how to operate the ship. There were places in the ship where it was difficult to breathe. There were times when the whole ship would shake, knocking us to the ground."

"How long did the journey take?" Brynne asked.

"We don't keep time the same way you do. We worked when we were told to work, and we stopped when we were told to stop, and we slept when we were told to sleep." Suski looked at me. "You've noticed I do not sleep as much as others do. It's how I've been trained."

"For me, it was possibly fifty sleeps," Coya said.

Rachel bit off a piece of cracker. "And you were told you were going home?" She looked at me and Brynne. "Maybe they were able to program the autopilot to take them back to the planet they'd come from. Maybe there was something in the computer that reminded them of home, and they were able to select a course here?"

"Possibly," Suski said. "We do not know. Perhaps my father knew. Perhaps someone in the tents knows."

"The computer would have to have some record of where they'd been," Rachel said. "Maybe there were even slaves who were forced to work on the bridge, and they observed enough to pilot the ship."

"I do not think there was a pilot," Coya said. "It did not seem like it. I think the ship directed us."

"Either way," Brynne said with a smile. "I'm claiming you guys as my science thesis."

"You were abducted from lands not far from here. We can go to them soon, so you can see, although you won't remember. Maybe you'll have stories. But maybe all you had to do was tell your computer to return you to your home planet, and it did."

"Possibly," Suski said.

My grandma was gone for a long time—long enough that

we lay down on the blankets on the floor and did our best to sleep. The hogan held in the heat well, and I was warmer when Rachel rolled over and put her back against mine. Suski didn't sleep, but sat by the fire, staring through the grate into the stove. He kept it stoked with wood—fire was a new concept to him, and I could tell he found it fascinating.

I listened as one by one everyone in the room began to breathe more slowly and drift away. I thought about Coya as I watched her sleep, about the life that she'd come from, trying to lead people who had all accepted the reality of their own deaths. I thought about Suski, who had to have been involved in the mutiny—he was Mai's son.

I felt a funny sort of comfort that horrible things happened everywhere, not just here on Earth. The Masters were bad—so bad that it made Earth, with all its problems, seem peaceful and welcoming. It felt like, if we could just get rid of the Masters, then everything was going to be okay. I knew it wasn't as easy as that, but that night in the hogan it felt that way.

And I felt safe. Like there was something about the hogan that was keeping the evil at bay—something about the fire, or the steeped tea, or the patterns in the wool rugs. We didn't have a lock on the door, but I felt safer there than I had the entire drive from Minnesota.

The aliens hadn't attacked. That meant one of two things. They either couldn't attack, which was unlikely, or they were waiting. Perhaps they didn't know where we were.

And at some point, when Suski had finally dozed off and the fire started to die down, I fell asleep.

When I awoke there was coffee brewing on the stove—harsh, black stuff that my grandma always made and I'd always been too young to try. This morning she handed me a cup, though, and coaxed me up. She had metal cups for Brynne and Rachel, too. Kurt was already standing, a bundle of newly chopped cedar in his arms. He laid it in a neat pile where Grandma showed him.

"Where are Suski and Coya?" I asked, getting up to my knees.

"Outside," Grandma said. "With the Elders."

I rubbed my face and dug through Brynne's bag for a hoodie. I found one with "National Science Foundation" embroidered on the chest. "Nerd," I said with a yawn.

"You're the one wearing it," she replied, sipping at the coffee and making a face.

All of my friends were asked to leave the hogan except for me—Brynne and Rachel gave me smiles of encouragement, and the Guides and Elders joined us. The chief singer took a seat on a buckskin and an even older man stood, his frailty showing in his trembling hands, but not on his firm-set jaw and wrinkled face. This man was not Navajo. He was Hopi—I could recognize it in the features of his face and the clothing he wore. He must have driven all night to get here.

"It is said that long ago our people were taken from us," he said. "This is not sung in the songs and not recorded in the histories. It is told from father to son—a knowledge that will save our people one day. I have traveled from my home in the Waalpi, First Mesa, to pass on this knowledge. All of the Elders here know the stories."

A man started to sing, low and quiet, as he pulled materials from his bag.

The Elder continued speaking while the other man worked. "It is said that monsters came from the sky, a thousand generations ago. Benny Selestewa's grandfather's grandfather was digging for a well out by Chaco Canyon. He found this." He patted the back of the man who was unwrapping the package. "Benny is Hopi. He has been given his weight to bear."

As the Elder spoke he began a sandpainting, drawing with black sand. He drew for what seemed like hours, alternating talking and singing. I had heard once that a Navajo *hata'lii* had memorized the equivalent of all of Shakespeare's plays. Never once did he falter in his singing or painting, never did he even take a rest.

Benny Selestewa spoke. "It is said they could travel faster than our fastest horses, higher than the highest eagle. They were powerful, with knives that could kill with an eyeblink and guns that fired the sunlight. And they took many of our people before we learned a way to fight back."

The other man had taken a mano and metate from his bag—a sort of mortar and pestle for grinding corn—only he was smashing juniper berries and dried insects and the buds of dried flowers I didn't recognize.

"We learned how to kill the monsters," Benny said. "And they left. It was too late for our people, but they left us enough to pick up the pieces."

His small sandpainting was done. It was stylized, but the shape was obvious. He had drawn one of the alien spacecraft. I gasped when I recognized it. The old man pulled out a heavy burlap bag from behind him at the wall. He set the bag down on the sandpainting and slowly began unpeeling layers of dusty cloth. It looked like this object hadn't been unwrapped in ages—perhaps even in lifetimes. Maybe it had even been buried.

With each piece of cloth that came off, I was closer to understanding what lay beneath the wrappings.

Dread filled my stomach, and Suski and Coya leaned forward to see.

The last strip of cloth was unwound, revealing a browned, tarnished bone. Coya recoiled, hands to her face, as the cloth fell away from the package. It was the skull of a Master. It was covered with horns—some broken and some still razor sharp. It looked like the head of a monster. It *was* the head of a monster.

The singer stood up and blessed all who were there, casting corn pollen at us and drizzling it on the ancient skull.

I watched Suski's face—it was one of bitter anger and fierce resilience. He took his sister's arm and pulled her back. And then he surprised all of us by spitting at the skull. He covered the microphone with his hand and said something to Coya that the translator couldn't hear to process, and after a moment of coaxing she, too, spat on the skull.

"We have vowed to watch for the return of our people," Benny said. "And now you have come."

Another man, who introduced himself as Orlando, said, "We will shield you from the dangers of the monsters just as Monster Slayer saved his people from his people's enemies—Monster Who Kills with His Eyes, Monster Who Kicks People Down the Cliff, Monster Eagle."

"But how?" Suski asked, letting go of his translator. "They are very strong."

"The People are stronger," Orlando said, and he pointed to the man mixing ingredients in his mano and metate. "An arrow."

Another ancient man reached forward with an arrow—its shaft as straight and strong as any I'd seen in my former private school's archery class, but this was made from wood and fletched with real feathers. The arrowhead was obsidian.

The old man scraped the arrow into the metate and then

back again, gathering a coating of the mixture on both sides of the tip.

"We learned their weakness," the man said to Suski. "We know a poison that will kill them with a touch. It has been a secret passed down from generation to generation."

And then he looked at me. "You are fortunate to have such a wise grandmother. She was aware of these traditions, of the old ways."

The man in the back reached forward with two full quivers of arrows.

"We will prepare ourselves," the old man said, and then to me, "You know how to call them here? Our Elders have seen it."

I was flustered by everything I had just heard, by the horrific skull lying on the floor, but I nodded my head. "I know how to call them."

The gathering of the Elders was gone—packed up and left in much less time than I could have thought possible. Instead, when I went outside to Brynne, Rachel, and Kurt, I saw a stunning sight. Twelve men—adult men, in their twenties—dressed in full traditional garb and waiting on horseback. They barely acknowledged us as we left the hogan and went around the back of Grandma's house to where Bluebell waited. We had maybe two more hours of sunlight—the ceremonies had lasted all day. The four of us pulled the tarp off her, and I didn't even bother to check for scratches, so consumed was I with what was ahead of us.

Brynne, Rachel, and Kurt dug through their bags for their phones, replacing SIM cards and batteries. I plugged the GPS fuse back in and then sat down in the driver's seat. I let out a slow breath and started her up. She purred to life in that quiet, beautiful way that well-cared-for BMWs do, and I waited for the GPS screen to activate.

"I've got one bar," Brynne announced. "Probably roaming charges out the wazoo."

"Text someone," I said.

"Already on it."

"I've got two bars," Kurt said. "Looking up the news now."

The GPS slowly connected with the satellite and found us—it didn't recognize us as being on a road and thought I was off in the bushes. That was okay. It had found us. That was all it had to do.

Kurt spoke. "The ship tried to attack the tent city," he said. "It shot down two aircraft and disappeared. Witnesses say that it was hit again. A missile or something."

"So they're injured," I said. "They'll be looking for an easy target."

"I just hope we're not too easy," Kurt said.

I reached out and took his hand, and he squeezed mine back.

"Emily says, 'OMG, I thought you were dead,'" Brynne said. "So if that's the trigger, we've got it covered."

"Let's get to a place they know," I said, pointing to the rocky mesa behind. I called out to the men on horseback. "We're going to Chaco Canyon."

I drove slowly, keeping the riders in sight off to my right.

"Phones?" I called out to everyone in the car.

"Yep," Brynne and Kurt said. As we entered the Chaco Canyon National Monument—it was only a few miles from *Shimasani*'s hogan—Rachel finally got a signal on her phone. She texted her parents to let them know she was okay, and then once again opened the phone and pulled out the battery.

"So we just wait?" Kurt asked. "I texted my girlfriend."

My phone buzzed.

"Whaaat?" Brynne said, all grins.

"Very slick, Kurt," I said. "And, yes, we just wait," I said, feeling my breathing constrict a little under the weight of what lay before us. I stopped the car at Pueblo Bonito, the biggest and most preserved of the ruins in the canyon.

I turned in my seat and looked at Suski beside me and Coya in the back. "So, do you want to see where you're from?" Behind us, to my right, I could see the dust plume of the men following on horseback.

"This pueblo is shaped like a D," I said, making a D with my hand. "The straight edge goes perfectly straight to the east over hills and arroyos until it hits another Chaco ruin—Pueblo Pintado. But that's nothing—they don't line up with the sun—they line up with the moon at the end of its fourteen-year cycle."

"I didn't know the moon had a fourteen-year cycle," Brynne said.

"Neither did I," Rachel said, her brow furrowing.

"I'm getting the Bruner Award in knowing about the moon's cycle. And that's just the beginning. They have some amazing astronomical charts on Fajada Butte. Stuff that makes Stonehenge look like child's play." I pointed to the round mesa to our southeast. "Seriously, I think that your people had a very good reason to pay attention to outer space."

"Guys," Kurt said, "we're in trouble. It wasn't just that one Master ship. There are now reports of eight of them over the Guide ship. It looked like they were taking it over—opening doors on the top and going inside. But they all just left, heading west. Toward us."

The horsemen were weaving in and out of the ruins, watching the sky but checking the corners. They each held a bow in one hand, and had a holstered rifle hanging down from the saddle.

We left Bluebell on the road—running, just in case.

I didn't know what was on those arrows, but I hoped that the recipe for the poison hadn't deteriorated over the course of a thousand years or so. It was all oral tradition—they had the skull, but it didn't seem like they'd written down the ingredients. Could arrows even penetrate that heavy reptilian skin?

I guess that wasn't our problem. We were just supposed to be bait. We didn't have weapons. We ran around the back side of Pueblo Bonito to where a rockfall had smashed through the four-story walls. The massive stones had been made into an ideal photography spot for tourists, but it gave us a great vantage point to watch for the Masters, three stories up, overlooking the pueblo.

Suski and Coya were taken into the ruin, into a center room with high walls, guarded by the Navajo riders.

Unless they came down the cliff wall behind us.

And then Rachel screamed.

EIGHTEEN

I spun around, facing the last remnants of daylight, and saw Rachel being lifted off the ground by one of the Masters. The entire ship was right there in the flat open expanse of Pueblo Bonito's plaza—we hadn't noticed it coming or landing—it hadn't even made the slightest breeze. It was just right there—and one of the creatures had Rachel.

Four Masters had emerged from the ship, two of them standing right in front of us.

"We aren't armed," I said.

"Then you're as stupid as you are weak," the translator said.

Rachel was bleeding profusely from the shoulder. She was tall, but looked small in comparison to this mammoth beast.

The other nearby Master had a gun—a wicked-looking

thing with three barrels and a stock that wrapped around his hand and wrist, all the way up to his twisted, bony elbow. The gun was pointed at me. In another hand he held a foot-long knife, and he was twirling the blade eagerly.

"We're not who you're looking for," I said. I didn't say it to pass the buck. I just knew that the riders had the magic poison, and we had nothing. They had to get a good shot, and quickly.

"You're trying to hide my animals," he bellowed.

Immediately, Kurt stepped in front of me, and the Master swung out one of his four arms and knocked him away. I saw a flash of blood, and then Kurt hit a two-story wall and flipped over the top of it. He landed on the other side with a cry of pain.

I tried to keep my eyes locked on the Master, but they were filling with tears. Kurt had to be okay. He had to be.

"Let her go," I said, gesturing nervously at Rachel.

He dropped her, but then grabbed her with another arm as she fell, his claws digging into her abdomen. She shrieked.

"Why are you doing this?" I screamed. I needed to make noise. I needed the horsemen to hear me. "Why can't you leave us alone?"

I saw one of the riders lining up a shot, but a blast of blue light hit his horse and the rider went down.

"Do you know what your friends have cost my people?" the Master replied. He tossed Rachel onto the ground, into the dust and sage. She writhed in pain. Brynne ran to her. I stood transfixed.

"Do I know what they cost *your* people?" I said. "What about what *you* cost *my* people?"

Another man was off his horse and standing on a wall, pulling back his bowstring.

"What do you mean 'your people'? These slaves were taken from this weak little planet more than eight hundred of your Earth years ago. We took only what we needed—we bred the rest. Your population is exploding. You seem to have more than enough to spare a few."

"We care for all our people," I said.

An arrow hit him in the back, and he reached around and pulled it out.

"You're fighting us off with sticks and stone?" My stomach fell right down through my shoes. The poison didn't work.

But then the Master took a deep, raspy breath. "You care for all people," he said with a cough. "If that were true, then why do you have wars? Poverty? Preventable illness? No, I don't think you care for all your people very much at all."

"And I'm sure you're perfectly peaceful," I said, Pissed-Off Alice taking over for Scared Alice.

"We do not have wars with our own people," he said. "We share our wealth."

A second arrow struck, this time in the arm. "You care for the poor and weak?"

"Wrong!" he rasped. "We do not have poor and weak. We only have strong. So we must find weak to implant and use."

"And you don't see anything wrong with that?"

"It is only nature." His green reptilian coloring was turning decisively gray.

"I've seen a different kind of nature. A nature that cares for the sick. That fights for its friends."

"And you can see how well it's gone," he said. He took a step toward me.

There was nowhere I could go to back up. There was a twenty-five-foot drop behind me.

"Sometimes death is inevitable," I said, echoing Suski's words. "But I've protected my friends the best that I know how."

"And it isn't good enough," he said.

Suddenly, the second Master—the one with the gun and knife—bellowed and reeled back. He pointed his gun and fired toward the path. Rocks exploded in a flash of light and flame. He fired again and again, some of his shots hitting the mesa top and some flying off into the night.

He was still bellowing, shouting something in his garbled language. And then he fell to one knee.

I could see the arrow, buried halfway up its shaft into his chest.

The other two Masters were moving out toward the cover of kivas and walls.

"What is this?" the one in front of me snapped, and he slashed his claws at me, but there was no strength left in him.

Another Master swung two arms' worth of claws at me. Something darted in front of me, and it changed his swing just enough that instead of plunging deep into my shoulder, his claws dragged across my chest and collarbone.

I screamed at the white-hot pain, but he was screaming, too, bellowing in a raspy alien cry.

And then he grabbed at me, his claws scraping around the traditional velvet shirt my *shimasani* had dressed me in. He yanked me forward, dragging me toward him through the brush.

Someone shouted something in Navajo, and then I was in his arms, held up like a human shield.

More guns were fired, but all I could see were the explosions as rock flew into the sky.

Dark shapes were appearing all around the plaza, arrows pointed at the Master. Another Master fired his gun and a great gout of flame erupted from the wall. Arrows flew back. There was a scream, but I couldn't tell if it was anger or pain.

"What is this?" the Master carrying me repeated, as one of his many arms yanked an arrow free from his body.

I could hardly breathe, he was holding me so tight against his chest. His long claws pierced my skin and I felt blood dribbling from my body.

He dropped the arrow, and I tried to snatch it out of the air, to have some kind of weapon. But it slid through my fingers and only barely touched my shoe.

"Let me go," I said.

He laughed, but his laugh was screechy and enraged.

"Let me go," I said again. "You're already dying."

"I cannot be killed by a simple stab," he said. "But you can."

He clenched his fingers tighter against my body and I shrieked as the claws pierced deeper.

I reached a hand, slowly so he wouldn't notice, into the waistband of my skirt. My fingers felt for the pistol grip of the Taser. I'd pulled it out of the car, although I hadn't thought I would need to use it. Now it was my only hope.

Gingerly, I pulled it free. Fighting against the pain in my chest, I held it the way the FBI agent had shown me. I pointed it under my arm—almost at point-blank range. I wondered if that would even work. Would I shock myself? Either way, it would make him drop me.

I pulled the trigger, and the Taser fired its darts.

The Master shivered and then shouted, "Some crude weapon? It will not work."

He swiped his hand down, knocking the Taser from my

fingers—it felt like he'd broken my hand, and I cried out.

I'd failed.

The bowmen were climbing onto the walls, circling us. I could only assume that the other Masters had already been shot down, or they'd be shooting back.

"Leave us, or the girl dies!" the Master bellowed.

I saw Suski crest the hill, his white skin glowing in the darkness.

The Master saw him, too. "Bring the slave boy to me. I'll trade you the girl for the boy."

"No," I said, and tried to free myself, but the pain of his claws seared into me.

Suski walked toward us.

"No, Suski," I said, desperate. "Don't do it. He'll kill you."

Suski kept walking. He was wearing his headset, the speaker dangling from his shoulder, but he wasn't carrying any bow or arrow.

"He'll kill you," I said. "He knows he's dying. He only wants revenge."

Suski was right in front of us now, standing, waiting.

"Suski," I said. But there was nothing else to say.

The Master dropped me, and I turned and grabbed at him, trying to bend his arm into a jujitsu pain lock. But I was far too injured to do anything. He caught me by the neck and flung me to the ground, and then he stretched out an arm and seized Suski.

"You will pay for what you slaves did to my people," the Master said.

But then he growled in a low, guttural grunt. Suski murmured something, too quiet to hear or for the translator to pick up.

I saw Suski withdraw a knife from the Master's stomach—a black obsidian blade with a wood-carved handle. It was dripping in blood. Suski stepped back and then a half dozen arrows cut through the air and plunged into the Master.

I watched him fall to his knees as the life drained out of him. He clutched at his scaly chest, weakly tugging at the arrows that were buried in his skin.

Suski's white face glowed in the darkness as he knelt over me.

"Make sure they're all dead," I gasped. "Check the ship. And where are the other ships?"

"But you're hurt."

"I'll be fine," I said, hoping it was true. I could feel blood soaking all down my chest.

Coya was the next one to reach me, and I yelled at her to go help Rachel. She took my hand for half a moment and then ran. Someone else tried to help me and I told him to go help Kurt, but this one didn't listen—he scooped me up in his arms and began lifting me through a window in the wall to where another warrior stood. I was in terrible, searing pain. I looked for Kurt and Rachel as I was carried back to the road, but didn't see them, and I shouted at the Navajo man carrying me that we needed to go back and find them. He ignored me.

"Where are the other ships?" I insisted. "There will be more."

Grandma came running, and the Elders swarmed us. I kept telling them that they needed to help the others more, and they assured me they would, but no one seemed to be moving. The man carried me to the back of Grandma's truck, laying me on her blankets. She knelt beside me and pulled away the strands of torn cloth from my shoulder and chest.

The man who was carrying me pointed with his chin toward the sky to the south. The sky was full of explosions and trails of smoke. "From Kirtland Air Force Base in Albuquerque."

"Alice," a voice called. I turned away from Grandma's face to see Kurt lying beside me. His leg was raised and was being bandaged.

"Are you okay?" I said, tears starting to run.

"Broken leg," he said, his voice muffled. "Broken nose. Hopefully that's all. You?"

"It'll be a while before I wear a strapless gown again," I said, forcing a laugh. "Rachel's hurt bad." Soon, we were driven the few miles back to *Shimasani*'s hogan, and with every bump I felt like I was going to die.

We were brought into the hogan, Rachel first—she

looked bad—carried by Suski. Brynne had pulled off her own shirt and was using it to put pressure on Rachel's wounds. Grandma pulled her away, gave her a shawl, and then began examining the deep gouges across Rachel's body. She gave the men in the room a few orders in Navajo, and they rushed off to fulfill her demands.

Brynne came to me and checked my cuts.

"It's not bad, right?" I asked.

"It's not bad," she agreed, starting to cry herself. "So you can quit blubbering."

Grandma and two of the men worked on Rachel. I couldn't see much except for her bare stomach and a whole lot of blood. She was going to be okay. I knew it. She had to be okay.

Coya came into the room, followed by Suski.

"They're all dead," Coya said. "All four of them. We checked the spaceship. It's empty."

I looked at Suski. "What does this mean? Will they leave us alone now?"

He shook his head. "I do not know." He sat down on the blanket by my head. His fingers gingerly felt the slashes across my shoulder. "I doubt it."

I turned to Brynne. "Your phone worked down here. Can you get it for me?" She nodded and stood up, jogging out of the house.

"You were very brave, Alice," Suski said. "We heard you

talking to the Master as we entered the pueblo."

"I was stalling for time," I said.

"It worked. It gave us the chance to surround them."

"You guys were the brave ones," I said. "You fired the arrows."

"You defended your friends. And I didn't shoot an arrow. I don't know how."

I smiled, and he touched my face with the backs of his fingers. He was the brave one—he had come running into danger when I was in trouble. I don't think he knew what that meant.

A helicopter came for Rachel. It wasn't until they were hauling me out, too, and then Kurt, that I realized it wasn't a Life Flight medical helicopter—it was a large army helicopter, and there were two more of them that landed next to the spaceship. Brynne stayed with my grandma, and Coya and Suski, too. The helicopter took us to Albuquerque, where we landed on the roof of the hospital.

I got stitches—a lot of them. Three claws' worth. A plastic surgeon was called in to do the work, partially because of the location—across my chest—and partially because I was a VIP. Maybe normal people just had to deal with big alien scars on their chests, but not if you just helped fight off the War of the Worlds.

Every doctor wanted to hear the story, and I didn't know

how much I was supposed to keep private. But I heard Rachel spilling everything under the effects of morphine, singing part of it, and talking a lot about Brynne, a ghost who only Rachel could see. So I figured I'd better give them some straight answers. I tried to get through the story, constantly interrupted by nurses doing this and that, and phlebotomists taking my blood and administrators coming in to give their VIP condolences.

Kurt had a compound fracture to his tibia. I hadn't realized it was compound—he was good at not freaking out. Better than I would have been if I'd been thrown over a two-story wall and had the bone sticking out of my leg. But the doctors set his leg and stitched him up, and then put a cast on. They wouldn't bring him into my room, but I told them if I didn't see him soon I was going to get up and go hobble to his room by myself. They either took me more seriously or increased my painkillers. Either way, I felt like I was getting results.

It was Rachel I was most worried about. The shoulder wound, I was told, was all muscle. But the wound in her side included gouges in her liver and kidney and intestines. I was told the best trauma surgeons in the city were working on her, but I didn't want the best trauma surgeons in the city—I wanted the best surgeons in the world.

Eventually, Kurt's bed was wheeled in next to mine.

"Hey," I said.

"Hey."

"I want to make one thing perfectly clear. No more getting thrown around."

"Let's try to stay away from all alien-oriented excitement for a while," he said.

"No more injuries," I said. "Alien or not."

"So who were they tracing?" Kurt asked, staring at the ceiling. He seemed to be in a lot of pain.

"Off the phones? Who knows. Maybe it was more Bluebell than the phones."

"Where did that name come from?" he asked, clenching his painkiller pump.

"Bluebell? I wanted a dog."

"You want a dog and your dad buys you a sixty-thousand-dollar car?"

"Try eighty," I said. "And it wasn't my dad. My grandparents. They thought I'd be a lonesome homebody if I got a dog."

"Someone should tell them about the trouble you get into with that car."

"Maybe someone should," I said. "You want to meet them? I mean if you don't already have plans for Christmas."

"You're inviting me to the ancestral Goodwin homeland?"

"Christmas is coming," I said. "If you don't have any other plans."

"I'll cancel," he said. "Christmas for me is a lot of cash

presents, and then my parents have business meetings."

"It's settled then."

I sat up in the bed, testing my balance in my drug haze. I seemed okay. I pulled my IV cart along with me and lay down in the bed next to him. It was probably at least as uncomfortable for him as it was for me. Some alarm started to go off—I'd knocked something loose.

"This is an inauspicious beginning," I said.

"And just FYI," he said. "My leg hurts like a son of a bitch."

I smiled. "I wasn't planning to make out with you. I just want to lie down next to you. You're comfortable."

He tried to put his arm around my shoulder, but that's where all the stitches were. Instead he just took my hand.

A nurse came in, looked on disapprovingly, and then moved my cart closer and reattached the wires that monitored my heart.

"How long before your dad gets here?" she asked.

"At least four hours," I said.

"Then I want you out of there in three. Nurse's orders."

"Gotcha."

Rachel got out of surgery sometime while I was asleep, but when Kurt woke me up and told me that my dad would be here soon, we still hadn't heard any news about her other than that the surgery was over for today and they had more surgery scheduled for tomorrow. I kissed Kurt—just quick and gentle (actually long and lingering)—and I climbed back into my bed, purposefully unhooking some of the cables attached to me, so the nurse at the nurses' station would think I was dead. It brought her in quickly, and I pressed her for information about Rachel. She said that she couldn't give that information out because of government regulations, but that Rachel was in stable condition and sleeping.

Kurt must have had some sixth sense for things, because my dad came running in the door less than ten minutes later.

"Aly," he said.

"You came here," I said. "Instead of going to see the spaceship."

"They're all waiting for me out there," he said. "But I'm a big important person with a big important daughter." He inspected the bandages. "You got this from an alien?"

"I did."

"Pretty cool. Exclusive club. Only you and the president and a couple Secret Service agents can claim that."

"And Rachel," I said. "I need you to go flash your badge and find out how she is. Ask about her organs." I started to cry. "If she gets to keep them or if she's in real trouble." *Stop it, Goodwin.* I wiped away the tears and said, "I'm fine."

"I'll do it," he said, and kissed my cheek, squeezing my hand until I could get myself back together again.

Dad turned to Kurt. "You must be the boy I keep hearing about."

"I guess so," Kurt said.

"Well, Kurt," Dad said, "just remember that I specialize in tying things to rockets and sending them into space. And sometimes they accidentally blow up."

"Dad."

"You'll have no reason to kill me, sir."

"Kurt. You make sure she doesn't cry, okay?"

Dad smiled happily at Kurt and then sagely at me. "Let me go find out about Rachel for you."

It wasn't long before Dad came back in with news of Rachel. She'd had major surgery on her abdomen, but it looked like everything could be saved, with the exception of a small portion of intestine that they'd had to remove. She was scheduled to have reconstructive surgery on her shoulder in the morning. So far, no complications.

"She was tough, Dad," I said.

"It sounds like you all were."

EPILOGUE

Brynne won the Bruner, of course. And she graduated early and got a full ride to Stanford. She turned it down and took a fellowship at the University of Minnesota where she could help them build their genetics program with fifty-five thousand test cases on their doorstep.

In a move that created enormous controversy, the government stepped in and used eminent domain to take over somewhere in the neighborhood of five thousand acres of prime farmland—much of it the land that had been churned over when the ship crashed—and built housing, schools, and technical colleges. I was glad I wasn't in the middle of that debate.

I did get a little press for a while, which was fun. I went on the talk show circuit. Ellen and Jimmy Fallon were a lot more fun than Rush Limbaugh, but that's not any big surprise. I even got to go on that middle-of-the-night UFO conspiracy radio show. But things settled down for me eventually.

Rachel recovered, and when the time came to award Bruners, they announced that she had achieved the first perfect math score ever. She wasn't going to graduate early—she was still going to be my roomie for another year—but a lot of colleges were spending a lot of time and money wooing her. William broke his hand punching his dorm door.

Rachel's parents also paid to sponsor Coya and Suski as students at Minnetonka—and they even found a Keresan speaker who could be their personal translator and English tutor.

That just leaves Kurt. And what is there to say about Kurt? We spend a lot of time sitting on the couch, studying or surfing the web, or enjoying a fire under a cozy blanket. Because it's warmer. Get your mind out of the gutter.

AUTHOR'S NOTE

Every effort has been made to create a book that both tells a good story, but also is respectful of the tribes and ancestors of tribes mentioned in the book. I have spread the manuscript out to people, both Native American and other tribal experts, and I've received feedback, both positive and negative. It is my hope that I've corrected the things that were in error or offensive.

I used to live on the Navajo Reservation. I bring this up not to say that gives me a free pass to write anything I want to that's Indian-related, but rather to say that I have enormous respect for The People. You may have noticed in the book that many people have different words for Native Americans: Indians, Native Americans, or American Indians. I purposely didn't choose a single description, even though I know some of these terms make some of the groups angry. Why? Because when I lived on the reservation, I heard Navajo men and women refer to themselves by all these labels. My preference is for the mostly Canadian term *First Nations*. It seems to be an all-around better, more respectful and honest term.

The reason I decided to choose Keresan as the language the Guides spoke was artistic license—and also hedging my bets: Keresan is spoken by many people in many tribes. In other words, it gave me a little more leeway to work with the language.

Speaking of Anasazi, that's the curmudgeon in me. When I lived on the reservation, we called the ancient people *Anasazi*. When I went to college and briefly majored in anthropology, we were taught that *Anasazi* was offensive (some people say that *Anasazi* was a Navajo word for "ancient enemy," which is offensive if you are the descendants of those people). So we used the Hopi word *Hisatsinom*. But then the other tribes balked at that, arguing that they all were descendants, not just the Hopi, so they needed a better word. The academic world settled on *Ancestral Puebloans*. This book calls them Anasazi, for clarity's sake, although it does state that *Ancestral Puebloans* is more correct.

The small amount we see of the ceremony and meeting with the Elders is a very whittled-down version of a real Navajo ceremony. Originally we saw all of it, but the Navajos I spoke to—with only one exception—said it was too sacred to depict. I cut it back and back until they were satisfied.

I would like to thank Orlando Tsosie, Sammy Jim, Thomas Begay, Angelina Begay, Nadine Padilla, Susie Sandoval, and Thomasita Yazzie. Their advice ran the gambit, but I've tried to incorporate all of their feedback, especially the negative feedback, and make this a book that is respectful of all tribes.

ACKNOWLEDGMENTS

Despite being my shortest book, this has been the hardest book to get right. But there are a few people I want to thank for sticking with me.

First of all: my editor, Erica Sussman. By rights, she must be so sick of this book. We've worked on it enough that she can probably quote it. But she has hung with it (and me) and always with a smile. Or at least a little emoticon smiley. Those little emoticons keep me going. :)

And right there with her is Stephanie Stein, Erica's associate editor. I'm always amazed at how these two ladies know my book better than I do, and can spot tiny continuity problems chapters and chapters apart. Anyway, they are an amazing team.

I need to thank my wife, Erin, who has to walk the fine

line of being honest in her critiques and living with me. She is critic, shoulder to cry on, psychologist, caregiver, religious counselor, best friend, love of my life, and so much more.

Big thanks to Sara Crowe, my ever-confident agent.

My readers: Patty Wells, Annette Lyon, Luisa Perkins, Krista Jensen, Jenny Moore, Josi Kilpack, Nancy Allen, Lu Ann Staheli, Sarah Eden, Jeff Savage, Michele Holmes, Heather Moore, Evelyn Hornbarger.

And to Annie, who is the best. The best.

Also from Robison Wells

"I loved it! The twist behind it all is my favorite since ENDER'S GAME."
—James Dashner, *New York Times* bestselling author of the Maze Runner trilogy

TRUST NO ONE.

VARIANT

ROBISON WELLS

Follow the rules.
Stay off their radar.
Trust no one.

THEY ARE NOT ALONE.

FEEDBACK

Sequel to VARIANT

ROBISON WELLS

Don't miss a
single page of the
pulse-pounding
Variant series.

www.epicreads.com